CHECKMATE

Checkmate

Sequel to the novel - Some Play Chess….

All rights reserved
Copyright © 2014 by Linda Wasylciw
Website: www.lindawasylciw.ca

No part of this publication
may be reproduced, stored or transmitted
in any form, or any means,
(electronic, mechanical, photocopying, recording or otherwise),
without the prior written consent of the copyright owner.

This book is a work of fiction.
All characters are fictional.

Also by Linda Wasylciw:

- The Twisted Spire
- Forgiveness….Be damned
- Some Play Chess…
- Perkins' Ghost

Some play chess,

others play bridge,

while a great many others

play the game of

recreational sex.

If the fish hadn't

opened its mouth,

it wouldn't have

been caught.

………..author unknown

CHAPTER ONE

KENNETH DANCED a little jig as he went up the stairs, moving in time to the music and smiling as he followed the trail of the scent of jasmine. He carried two wine glasses, one for himself and one for Jessica. He didn't think about the rocky times of their marriage, for in his mind they were trivial to say the least, if they had existed at all. At the remembered line in the song 'Memories' he joyfully sang along. He had never felt more elated. Jessica had finally realized that it was her female emotions that had disrupted their lives, her hormonal thing as he called it, and that their life had finally slipped back into its usual fashion. When he reached the top stair he recognized the heavy scent of jasmine and momentarily wondered why Jessica was not using rosewater. It was his favorite.

It also surprised him to see that the door to the master bedroom was open. They had not used that room for many months. After her 'incident' in Banff, as Kenneth referred to it, Jessica had moved into the guest room. And, when it was obvious that she wasn't moving back into the master suite, he had moved into the guest room with her. Over those months it became the bedroom they had shared. His heart raced and confusion rose inside him as he recalled the night when she had got lost in the woods in Banff.

Then at the sight of the candle-light, reflecting from the mirror, in the master en-suite, his heart rate settled. 'She must be preparing herself for this evening's dinner and having her bath in there,' he thought, sighing and recognizing it as another sign that things were better with her, with life, with them. Maybe that was her first step in moving back into the master suite? After all, she had always boasted that it was one of the loveliest rooms in the house. In his mind it was a shame that it wasn't used any longer.

The unused bedroom was neat as a pin. Kenneth stepped into the alcove, just as Jessica had done only an hour before him. He looked at the lights that twinkled on the open water on the pond that edged the river. Then he thought of Jessica, soaking in the bathtub. Added warmth was given to the room just by knowing that she was on the other side of the door, a feeling that was absent only yesterday. The c.d. player now changed songs and another favorite of Jessica's began, 'Tomorrow', the joyful kids' song from the stage-musical, Annie. He paused to listen and remembered how much Jessica had enjoyed that play. He smiled again before turning away from the window and walking into the en-suite.

Kenneth stepped across the threshold. In shock and in horror he dropped the two wine glasses. They crashed to the floor sending shards of glass around the room. Candlelight glinted from the splinters of glass and pools of wine, casting an eerie glow. Kenneth fell to his knees and felt as if he and the whole room were floating, drifting into outer-space. He knelt there frozen in shock, staring, unable to move. The bath water was a dark red, so much so that it was almost black in color. Jessica lay immersed in the bloodied water and her pale face lay against the sloped back of the tub. Her eyes were closed. There was a smile on her face.

Kenneth's scream echoed from the walls, "Noooooooooo." It was a long, hideous sound. He crawled across the room needing to be next to Jessica, to touch her. The fragments of glass cut into his hands and knees. He held Jessica's face in his hands, leaving streaks of blood across her pale skin. He kissed her lifeless lips.

He cried and mumbled, "Oh baby, why, why would you do this to us. I love you so much."

And he wept.

Time passed. The water cooled. Kenneth, for the first time ever, had a fleeting understanding of what Jessica had been saying for the past year.

He said to her, "I am so sorry. I didn't know. We could have stopped. *I* could have stopped. I didn't know. I love you so much. Please come back to me, I can't live without you."

But it was too late for his words, for she could not hear him. The last words that she had heard from him were of his expectations for the evening's dinner party, a party that she *could not, would not,* attend.

She had known that it was to be another evening of group sex. Although he hadn't actually said it outright, she knew what he had planned at the moment when he gave her the names of the guests.

At the ringing of the doorbell Kenneth dragged himself to his feet. The first of their dinner guests had arrived. Music still played from the stereo as Kenneth made his way to the front door. Droplets of blood dripped from the cuts on his hands leaving a trail from the en-suite, down the stairs and across the white tiles in the foyer. A dazed Kenneth opened the door for Peter and Gloria and the welcoming aroma of dinner drifted out into the night air from the roast-lamb that Jessica had so carefully prepared. She had ever so methodically laid the dining-room table to accommodate Kenneth and *his* four guests. Her own place setting had not been laid. The guests and police would later see this and better understand the situation.

Streaks of blood colored his fair hair where he had brushed his hands through it and there were red smudges on his face.

Peter was shocked and horrified at what he saw. He immediately wondered whether Kenneth had resorted to violence and asked, in horror, "Kenneth, what have you done?"

"No, no, it was Jessica. She did it."

Peter was uncertain what that meant and said to Gloria, "You stay here."

He followed the droplets of blood, racing up the stairs.

Gloria held Kenneth against her chest and cooed to him as a mother would her child. She and Peter had known Kenneth for more than a year and had met on many occasions, but they had only met Jessica that one time, in Montana, at the Callisto Akantha retreat. Gloria stared at the dark spots of blood in the foyer and on the steps. Questions floated around in her head as she wondered what Peter would find when he went upstairs. She listened. Peter was talking with someone but she could not make out who it was. Maybe Jessica *was* okay? She looked again at Kenneth and given his state she seriously doubted it. Then she heard Peter relaying an address, this address. 'He must be on the phone and talking with the ambulance people,' she thought.

Although Gloria had never been in this house before, she instinctively led Kenneth from the front door and to a chair in front of the fire. Kenneth slumped into the same wing-backed chair that Jessica had sat in earlier. He was mumbling words that were indecipherable, shaking like a man just brought in from the cold. He was weeping like a child.

The fireplace still had the remains of a fire and a small flame burned. Gloria looked curiously at the book, half burned, in the corner of the fireplace. As much as she wanted to pull it from the ashes she didn't. The book cover had the title 'Feelings'. It was then that she guessed at what Peter had found upstairs.

At the sound of the door-bell she jumped up and raced for the door. Gloria was comforted to see that it was Brian and Karen. In the distance she could hear emergency sirens. She momentarily uttered a silent prayer, hoping that they would not be arriving at this address, though she knew that she was hanging on to false hope.

"Thank God, it's you," Gloria said.

"What's going on?" Brian asked.

"It's not good," Gloria told them, not knowing what else to say.

"Where's Kenneth?"

"In the living room…... Jessica is upstairs," she said, looking upwards. She could see Peter pacing back and forth in the mezzanine area on the second floor. He was still on the phone.

Brian and Karen rushed to Kenneth's side. They stared in horror at his blood soaked hands.

Gloria looked at them and said, "It looks as if he was crawling around on broken glass," still wondering what possibly could have happened before their arrival. 'Was there a fight?' she wondered. They huddled around him, laying reassuring hands on his shoulder.

When the sound of the sirens grew louder Gloria moved to the door. She knew that they were coming for Jessica. 'Maybe she's okay', Gloria hoped. She opened the door and pointed for the paramedics to go up the stairs. The police arrived at the same time. They also followed the trail of blood up the stairs. Peter was still pacing but he was no longer on the phone. She wished that they could all go back out of the door, to start the evening again. She wanted to change the whole sequence of events.

Within minutes the paramedics were back down the stairs. A body had been laid out on the stretcher and was fully covered with a sheet. 'No, no', Gloria thought, 'Not Jessica.'

Minutes later the police officers returned to the foyer. One was holding a plastic bag with a small piece of paper inside it. They would later learn that the words, 'I love you Kenneth,' had been written by Jessica, on that piece of paper. It was the only evidence that they would collect. They did not see the remains of her books in the fireplace but if they had it would have made the situation even clearer.

"Kenneth Lund?" one officer asked.

"He's there in the chair," Gloria said, pointing to the living room.

The officer said to Kenneth, "Mr. Lund, we'd like to ask you a few questions."

Kenneth looked at him, dazed, "Yea… yea… sure."

"What time did you get home?"

"Around five thirty I guess."

"Did you and Jessica have a fight?"

"Oh no. We don't fight," he said, forgetting the many times over the past year when Jessica cried and begged him to stop all that sex stuff.

"There's glass all over the bathroom floor. What happened?"

"Jessica, my Jessica. I don't know," Kenneth said, weeping.

"How did you get those cuts on your hands?"

"I don't know," Kenneth said.

"Did you fight?" he asked again.

"No…. everything was perfect. We had friends coming to dinner."

The officer looked at Kenneth's hands and the cuts on his knees trying to visualize the sequence of events. It was obvious that they were faced with a suicide but the questions still had to be asked.

Another officer was going from room to room and entered the living room just as Kenneth mentioned the dinner party. "How many were coming to dinner?" he asked.

"Four," Kenneth wept even louder when he realized the truth of it all. The officer also understood as he looked at the five people in the living room knowing that Jessica had had no intention of *dining* with them that evening.

CHAPTER TWO

WHEN SYBIL and Nicholas returned to her apartment, from their Valentine's evening dinner, the telephone was ringing. She had, just that morning, told Jessica about Nicholas and their plans for a lovely, romantic dinner at a very expensive restaurant. Even though that was only their second, official date Sybil knew in her heart that she had finally found the man of her dreams.

She had intentionally left her cell phone at home, not wanting to be disturbed. She hesitated, not wanting to answer it, and looked inquiringly at Nicholas. At his nod she reluctantly picked up the call with an unwelcoming, "Hello."

"It's Jeffrey, Kenneth's partner," he said.

"Jeffrey? Why are you calling me?" she asked, surprised that he would call her and even more so at that hour.

"It's Jessica," he said, simply. "Please phone your parents."

"What do you mean 'It's Jessica'?" Sybil asked almost shouting.

"It appears that she committed suicide."

"*Appears*, what is that supposed to mean? That is not funny Jeffrey. How dare you say such a thing?" she said, clearly upset.

"I'm sorry Sybil."

She hung up the phone, looking wild-eyed and began crying. Nicholas held her tightly against his chest as she thrashed against him and wept. Eventually she settled and he released her. He took her face in both his hands and kissed her gently on her forehead.

"What can I do?" he asked.

"Just hold me, for now. I have to phone mum but I just don't know how to tell her."

Within hours of Jessica's death everyone had been notified including Jessica's and Sybil's parents in Prince Edward Island. From that moment forward their lives would never be the same.

As late as it was, Nicholas and Sybil drove over to see Sue who was babysitting Jessica's two children. Clarissa was waiting for them. This was not their first time together nor was it the first time to be talking about Kenneth and Jessica. In the past months they had actually spent more time talking about Kenneth and Jessica than anyone else. It had started when Jessica had spent almost four months on Prince Edward Island with her parents and even more frequently after she had got lost in the harsh, winter wilderness in Banff. They all knew that something was not right in their relationship but no one knew what to do about it.

Thank goodness that it was late enough that the children were asleep, for that would allow them time to plan what they would tell them. What does one say to a ten and a seven year old? How does one tell them that their mother had killed herself? How could it be worded so that the children would not be damaged forever?

Sue answered the door immediately. They held each other and wept while Nicholas shuffled his feet back and forth watching helplessly.

"Here, let me get us something to drink," Sue said, wiping away her tears.

She settled them before the fireplace and asked, "What happened?"

"Who knows anything for sure except that Jessica is dead," Clarissa said, crying.

"I don't get it. I was there, just this morning, and we were talking about happy stuff. She was preparing a special dinner," Sybil said.

"I thought the same thing. I drove up as you were leaving. She offered me a glass of sherry and we had a lovely chat. She told me that it was *all sunny days*," Clarissa said.

"Sherry at noon?" Sybil said, critically.

"Yea, she suggested it. And why not?" Clarissa stated defensively, "She said we were celebrating life."

"Or death? What the hell does that mean anyway, 'all sunny days'?" Sybil asked, accusingly.

"How am I supposed to know?" Clarissa said, crying even harder, "She said it…. not me."

"Come on now, we shouldn't fight," Sue intervened. "Jessica would be really upset if she knew we were arguing. We need each other more than ever now. Maybe she was saying goodbye?"

"I think you might be right. I thought it odd when she told me to take those new rug-hooking kits: one for Sybil and the other for me. I didn't argue because she seemed to be getting back to her old self again and I didn't want to upset her. She said that she and Kenneth wouldn't be doing rug-hooking anymore."

"She planned this," Sybil said. "By the looks of things she didn't have any intentions of doing anything anymore, not just with Kenneth, but with anyone. But why?"

"I fucking knew it. He was forcing her to do something that she didn't want to. Just let me get my hands on his cell phone. I'll find out what he's been up to…. That bastard," Clarissa said, vehemently. "Remember when Jessica was in the hospital and he couldn't stop fiddling with that damned thing? I'll bet you he's into some bad shit."

"Talking like that won't bring her back. It'll just make us all upset. Forget about Kenneth. Right now it's the kids who we have to think about," Sue said.

"Mum and Dad will be here tomorrow," Sybil said. "They can stay with me. I'm taking the children home with me tomorrow too. And I don't give a damn what Kenneth says about it either."

They all turned as Brianna walked into the room. "Where's mommy? I heard her calling to me," she said, still half asleep.

Sue was immediately on her feet, "Mama's not here love. I'm sorry if we've disturbed you sweetie. Here let's get you back into bed. It's very late," she said, holding her hand and shooing her back up the stairs.

"But mommy said that it was okay," she said, sleepily, "What did she mean?"

Sue wrapped her arms around Brianna, half carrying her up the stairs and hiding her tears. "She was just saying that she loves you and that it's okay if you have a lie-in because there's no school tomorrow my dear," she said, trying to smile as she tucked her back into bed.

When Sue returned to the living room no one said a word. They just looked at each other. Finally Sybil said, astonished, "She came and said goodbye to Brianna, didn't she?"

"Do you think that's possible?" Clarissa asked, astonished.

They moved closer together, held each other and wept, each wishing that they could have had a similar last visit from Jessica.

"How are we going to live without her?" Sybil asked, sobbing.

"It won't be easy," Clarissa said.

They stayed like that, grateful that they had each other. No one spoke another word as they thought about Jessica, her vitality and her passion in thinking that she was saving the world, one species at a time. It would be Clarissa who would tell their fellow members of the Blue Marble Club that Jessica was dead.

Tired as they were, no one wanted to leave. They just felt the need to be together. Finally Sybil said, "I best get home and prepare for Mum and Dad's arrival."

"If you want me to help I can. I won't sleep anyway," Clarissa said.

"Thanks, but Nicholas will give me a hand," she said, as Nicholas gave her an affirmative nod.

****

Gloria and Karen scraped the dinner, which Jessica had prepared, into the trash and tidied up the kitchen. Kenneth refused to leave the house even though Jeffrey practically insisted that he spend the night with them. He just stared at the edges of the burnt books in the fireplace, weeping and arched in a fetal position. He wouldn't allow anyone to clear the dining room table or to move a single thing that Jessica had last touched. Finally they left him alone and he moved to the family room and started playing the collection of c.d.s again. He stared at the painting that Jessica had made of them, old and grey, the way that she had envisioned how they might appear in their senior years. He stroked the hooked-rug that they had made together during their first cold winter in Alberta, wishing that he could turn back the clock and retie every stitch. When Kenneth found the energy to climb the stairs he didn't go inside the master bedroom but he stopped and locked the door to it. He felt that he would never step into that room again. He slept in the guest bedroom, as he and Jessica had in her last months.

Early the following morning the children were taken from Sue's house to Sybil's. No one asked Kenneth's permission or opinion and he didn't say anything one way or the other. Funeral arrangements were made, primarily by Jessica's parents and Sybil. The only thing that Kenneth wanted to choose was the urn for her ashes. He chose a long, slender, shiny vase, burgundy in color.

CHAPTER THREE

JESSICA'S SUICIDE left the family and friends reeling and grappling with the question as to the why of it all. It was a harrowing time and they wondered if there was something else that they could have done. Guilt surfaced, for each of them now recognized the warning signs that had not been heeded. Her death also stirred other emotions.

Sybil needed to feel loved and to have sex. She was glad that Nicholas insisted on staying with her and that night they did make love, but not in the way that they had in the past and not in the way that she had planned for their special Valentines evening. That night it was she who had initiated their sex. It was brutal and aggressive. She cried tears of sorrow as she ground hard against him. Sybil wanted more than anything in this world for her sister to be alive again.

As for Clarissa, she needed her husband Jerry to make love to her too. She, however, wanted slow, sensual love. But he wasn't interested in sex and even at her time of grieving he hadn't even bothered to wait up for her. When she snuggled up to him and stroked his cock he pushed her hand from him. She rolled away, curled up, hugging herself and wept.

Kenneth, for the first time in years, had no interest in sex. Nor did he feel the anger or betrayal that is common when one's spouse dies. Jessica's dying had psychologically brought him even closer to her and what she was feeling. He understood her more now than he ever had in his life. Yet he would never admit that Jessica's suicide was done out of despair.

The grandparents clung to Jessica's children, Brianna and Simon, as if they were life itself.

****

Jessica's funeral could not have been a sadder event. Her tall, slender, burgundy urn held her remains and stood next to her photograph on the table at the front of the church. The picture was one that Sybil had taken when they were last home in Prince Edward Island. Jessica had sat on a rock, at the seaside. She had her knees raised and her arms wrapped around them. She wore a wide-flowing, multi-colored summer dress. The wind was blowing her long, blonde hair from her face and her eyes were a sea-blue. There wasn't a dry eye in the congregation even before the first hymn was sung. Jessica's parents sat next to Sybil and Nicholas, with the children tucked tightly between them. Kenneth was at the opposite end of the pew leaning against the edge, with a wide gap between him and the rest. He had separated himself from them, almost as if he was from a different family.

Kenneth's parents, Janie and Bruce, were in the pew behind Jessica's parents. Sue, Clarissa and a few members of the Blue Marble Club were next to them. Alicia and Pascal entered after everyone else was seated. They sat near the back of the church and left as soon as the last hymn was sung. Kenneth did not see them enter nor did he see them leave. Not that he would have cared.

Days before the funeral Clarissa had placed a phone call to the premier's office. She wanted to let the premier of Alberta know that one of the members of the Blue Marble Club had died: the little perfect person who had loudly played a recording of Rimsky-Korsakov's 'Flight of the Bumblebee' during a recent demonstration to save the bees. No one noticed when the Premier, the chief politician in the province, wearing full black and a veil, entered Jessica's funeral service and sat near the back of the church, next to Alicia. She, like Alicia, never felt a need to announce her arrival, her presence or her departure. However it would be impossible for her to listen to Rimsky-Korsakov's tune and not to think of Jessica. She simply left a card, on the tray, for Clarissa. Jessica would be remembered by many.

It was a small crowd that had gathered to mourn someone who had affected so many around her with so much love. Yet, Jessica would not have wanted it any differently for she never looked for praise in whatever she had done. The love of her close friends and family would have been more than enough.

****

Kenneth's emotional state was erratic, to say the least, saying things that didn't make sense to anyone and talking about Jessica as if she had just stepped out to go shopping. Given his state, Jessica's parents and Sybil didn't even ask him about the children but decided that Jessica would have expected her parents to take the children home to her beloved Island. Maybe if they lived there for a time they would think of it as home and eventually call it that, as Jessica had. Kenneth had nothing to say about Brianna and Simon going back to PEI with their grandparents. In fact Kenneth had little to say about anything these days. He never left the house, moving from room to room and taking Jessica's tall burgundy urn with him. He talked with Jessica like he had never done before.

Sybil, Clarissa and Sue found time to get together for frequent visits. They gained comfort in each other's presence. But, regardless of the day of the week, the never ending question was inevitably made: 'Why?'

"I'd sure like to know what Kenneth did to Jessica to make her do this." Clarissa said, during one of these visits.

"I knew that he was up to no good but I had no idea that it would lead to this," Sybil added.

"He's clearly responsible yet he doesn't even show any signs of remorse. It appears that he's got a full dose of that *woe is me syndrome*," Sue said, astonished.

"What should we do?" Clarissa asked.

"What can we do? We can't bring her back," Sybil said, sadly.

"I think we should hire a private detective to follow him, to see what he does," Sue suggested.

"I think it's too late for that. What's done is done. Besides according to Jeffrey he doesn't do anything anymore. He doesn't even leave the house, not even for work," Sybil said, sadly.

"But he has to be held accountable," Clarissa said, venomously.

"One can hardly nail him for her suicide. Sadly she did that to herself," Sue stated.

"Yes, but he was the cause. I sure would like to know what he did to her that made her do it," Clarissa said, tears rolling down her cheeks.

"I think we all know the answer and we've milked that one to death. Remember that club or organization that they were in?" Sybil said, sighing.

"Right that Callisto Akantha thing….. I think we need a drink," Sue said, getting up.

"At least he didn't argue with Mum and Dad about taking the kids home," Sybil said.

"Yes, that was a surprise. It's almost as though he doesn't care," Sue said, serving the drinks. "Here's to us. At least if we stick together he hasn't won."

"We'll always be together… to us…. to Jessica," Clarissa said. "This is what she would have wanted: us to be together."

CHAPTER FOUR

BRIANNA AND SIMON settled effortlessly into life at their grandparents' home on Prince Edward Island. It was an easy transition for them and not far different from when they went there every summer for a visit. Except now they were going to a new school, in mid-term, and trying to make new friends. Happily it was a whole lot easier than changing schools in a big city like Calgary. They were welcomed as if they were always a part of the island.

Within days of their arrival Grandfather James took them for a walk. He took them by the hand and walked step-by-step around the same eight mile loop that Jessica used to run regularly when she was last home: up the slope from the sea, beside the pitch-and-putt golf and past their other grandparents' house. They, like Jessica in the early part of her visit, didn't stop in and say hi to them. And it didn't matter on that first day, for later their visits would be frequent. Instead they walked on to where the red-cliffs dropped into the Atlantic, around the unplanted potato and corn fields and back to where they now lived. From time to time, during their walk, they had stopped and cried, holding tightly onto each other. During the entire length of their walk Grandfather James told them how their mother loved the wind on her hair, the sun on her face, and reminded them of all the things that made Prince Edward Island special to her. For in his wisdom he knew that Jessica would not die in their hearts if they worked at keeping the memory of her alive. He talked of her every day. And together they wept. They never once complained about how long the walk was. In the months that Jessica had run that course it had become known as Jessica's Loop and now it would always be called that.

      They adapted to island life and soon they took on that same maritime glow that shone from Jessica every time that she had visited. It was the same radiance that she had worn in her youth. Visits between the grand-parents' homes swung back and forth like the pendulum of a clock and as hours ticked away to days, and days passed to weeks, they less and less frequently asked about their father. But when they did ask they were told that he needed time to heal, as they all did. He never phoned. The children doubted that he would ever come to the island and at times they wondered if they would ever see him again. They never asked if they would go back to Alberta. And in their hearts they didn't want to leave, for they felt that the island was now their home. It was Jessica's dream for them to think of the Island in the same way that she did. Maybe residing closer to both grand-parents and living that slow-paced, down to earth existence would allow them to grieve in a normal fashion, in a world away from the hurried life of the city and *The Lifestyle* which had killed their mother; though that was something that they would never know.

Grandfather James took them out fishing. They later dug in the red sand and collected shells while he sat on a rock watching their every move. They lived a life not far different from the one that Jessica had had when young. They dreaded the thoughts of the school term ending for that might mean that they had to go back to Alberta. They hoped that they would attend the same school in the fall but they were too afraid to ask.

One snowy morning a stranger stopped by for a visit: Patrick Rowan. He brought for them a puppy, a female puppy that was not more than six weeks old. It was a golden retriever. They sat quietly, shyly petting their new dog, and listening as Nana Janet and Patrick talked. Jessica's name was often mentioned and when they heard this they held each other's hands and were very quiet.

The likeness of Jessica in Brianna was so uncanny that many times Patrick felt as if the hands-of-time had been reversed and that he was a little boy again. More than once he almost called out Jessica's name, ready to ask if she wanted to go and play on the swings. The visit, though ever so sad, was yet necessary to gain some of the closure that Patrick sought. He had asked Jessica to stay on the island the last time that she was there, knowing that she and Kenneth were having major problems. He had had great, though unspoken, hopes. He looked gaunt with sorrow when he left the house.

Patrick, like so many others, was broken hearted that he would never see Jessica again. Other neighbors came in singles and couples to pay their condolences and to get to know the children better. In that island community the whole of the population, not just the grandparents, would raise Jessica's children, for that was the way islanders lived. It was more than a community. It was a place where families grew as one.

The moment that Patrick walked out the door Brianna and Simon were all giggles and smiles, clutching the puppy in their arms, hoping to bring a smile to Nana Janet's face. They jumped up and down asking, "What should we call her?"

Janet said, "Well, one has to choose a name very carefully for once she is named it will be her name forever."

The golden haired puppy lay at their feet as they discussed and discussed that topic. Grandfather James joined in the conversation. Suddenly Brianna raised her hand as if she was in school and said, "I've got it. I've got it….. We should call her Jessie."

The room went deadly quiet and all eyes were on Brianna. She picked up the little dog and nestled it against her neck. She said, "Mommy would like that."

They all nodded.

****

Kenneth surprised Clarissa one morning by telephoning her. "I'd like to join the Blue Marble Club," he said. There was no preliminary 'hello' or 'how are you'.

"Kenneth…..? Is that you….? Are you sure….?"

"Yes, I'd like to visit the Burrowing Owl's nesting site. I want to do an over-night like Jessica had done years ago."

"But I thought that you didn't like that stuff? You said that what she was doing was silly and frivolous."

"Please don't say it like that. I was wrong. I'd like to go now."

"Well *maybe* I can arrange something. But I'm not so sure about a membership. Your heart has to really be there."

"Okay, for now I'll take just the visit. I'm looking forward to that. Thanks," he said, surprising her even more. Clarissa could not recall the last time that he had thanked her for anything.

"I'll keep in touch," Clarissa said, hanging up the phone and wondering what the hell that had been all about. She immediately phoned Sybil.

"What is it?"

"Kenneth," Clarissa said, as if that explained it all.

"Oh my God, what's he gone and done now?"

"Meet me at *The Office* on Fourth Avenue. We'll both need more than one drink for this one."

Almost all the tables at the fashionable bar, ironically called The Office, were full. Clarissa had chosen this location for it was reasonably convenient for both of them. Sybil was already waiting for her and had taken the liberty of ordering them a bottle of wine. Two menus lay on the table.

"What's up?" Sybil asked.

"Kenneth, I think he's losing it."

"What do you mean?"

"He wants to do an over-night out at the Burrowing Owls' nesting location."

"What for? I remember him always saying that all that stuff was nonsense."

"You and me both. He sounded really odd. Like he's on drugs or something."

"The doctor did prescribe him an anti-depressant. Maybe that's it," Sybil suggested.

"I don't think so. I've had my share of those, and, trust me, he's acting really oddly. It's not just nerve-pills."

"So he's odd... what's new? He's always been a bit different. I was one of the stupid ones who thought that he was a good catch. Goes to show my standards," Sybil admitted, embarrassed.

"Speaking of...... how's the new guy?"

"Nicholas? Alright I guess. Actually he's more than alright," she said, nodding and smiling. "He might even be a keeper. But let me tell you, I have a whole new check-list after what Kenneth did to Jessica."

"What gets me is how and what he actually did to her? You and I both know that he's as guilty as they come."

"Oh yes, I know, but sadly only she would know the whole truth of it."

"How are Brianna and Simon doing?"

"Mum says that they're fine. I'm going out to the Island again this summer. Nicholas wants to go with me."

"Sounds like things are more than alright with you two." After a pause she said, "Say, why don't we pay Kenneth a visit? Just you and me."

"Are you kidding me? What for? That's the last place that I want to go. I'd be happier if he left the city."

"I'm just a bit curious about what he's up to."

"Why?"

"I don't know. I guess because he phoned me….. I phoned Jeffrey right afterwards and he said that Kenneth is now going to work every day and according to him he goes straight home every night."

"Really? That'll make for a change. In the last year that Jessica was alive he was out of town *on business* more weekends than he was home. He fucking makes me sick."

"Come on Sybil, we'll just stay for a few minutes. We can go right now."

"Tell you what snoopy pants. I'll probably regret this but we'll go tomorrow, with a clear head," she said, emptying her wine glass.

****

Contrary to what Jeffrey had said about Kenneth's always being in, Sybil and Clarissa rang the doorbell three times. They were about to walk away but jumped in surprise when he opened the door with a rush.

"Sorry, I was cooking dinner," he said.

Sybil and Clarissa looked at each other.

"Come in," he said, cheerily.

"We just thought we'd stop over and talk about setting up a time when you can go out to see the Burrowing Owls. I hope you don't mind that we just dropped in," Clarissa said.

"Mind? No, of course not. Jessica will be so pleased that you're helping me with this."

A quick glance told each other that they both had caught Kenneth speaking of Jessica in the present tense.

"Come into the kitchen," he said, merrily, as if they had taken to visiting every week.

He led the way past the living room that was unkempt and dusty, aside from the area around Jessica's favorite chair, in front of the fireplace. A fire had burned earlier but was now almost out, little more than a few sparks glowed. When they walked past the dining room they were surprised to see that the table was masked with dust and in the sunlight cobwebs glistened between the chandelier and candlesticks. It looked like a scene from Great Expectations. A grey dust on the tabletop appeared white in the afternoon light. The only place setting that was clean was where Kenneth sat. And at the opposite end of the table, where there wasn't a place setting, was the mark of a tiny circle left in the dust. Aside from those two things it looked as though the room was exactly as it was the night when Jessica had died with only the original five place-settings still laid. Another quick glance at each other confirmed that they both saw it. The last time that Sybil and Clarissa had been in the house was before the funeral to pick up the kids' personal belongings and to have them shipped back east. It surprised them that Kenneth had kept everything just as it had been.

"Glass of wine?" he asked, stirring a pot of sauce.

"Sure why not?" they said.

"Have a chair," he indicated for them to sit at the bar. Jessica's urn stood tall and shiny at the end of the counter. Both thought that it was an odd place to keep it but neither said anything.

"Tell me about the owls," he said seriously. "I've been reading Jessica's books and I think that I'm almost up to speed on them. Thanks, Clarissa, you don't know how much this means to us," he said, nodding at Jessica's urn and taking Clarissa's hands in his.

Clarissa felt like saying, "Us? You got a mouse in your pocket?" but she didn't. Instead she drew her hands away from his and gave Sybil another meaningful glance. She moved to the other end of the counter, settled back in her chair, half leaning against the wall and took a sip of wine. Maybe they would stay longer than they had planned? This was actually getting interesting. Kenneth was nuttier than she thought. His little side-show would give them plenty to tell Sue about.

Clarissa said, "Then you probably know that they nest in late March or early April and we're just on the cusp of that, so you might even see some baby chicks. They hang around here until late fall. As a member I have the option of going out for one session a year. I'm slotted in for late June but I suppose we can bump that up to May on the chance that you could see the chicks." Without thinking she said, "We could go out together one night," and immediately wondered why she would make such a generous offer.

She didn't notice Sybil's jaw dropping reaction to her offer. Sybil didn't comment. There would be plenty of time to talk later.

"Oh Clarissa, Jessica will be so pleased," Kenneth said.

'There! He said it again,' Clarissa thought.

Sybil, anxious to change the subject and to get the hell out of Jessica's house, never to come back, said to Kenneth, "Those rug-hooking kits. Jessica wanted us to have them."

"Super, I'll get them for you."

"I can help, if you like," Sybil said. She wanted to snoop a bit and followed him.

"Sure," he said as he stepped into the room off the kitchen. Months before her suicide Jessica had begun remaking Kenneth's old office space into an art studio, with thoughts of getting back into painting. That room was dusty as well. Kenneth took the package of rug-hooking kits off the shelf and handed it to Sybil. She took it and looked around the room. Sybil liked the color of paint that Jessica had chosen and it gave her a feeling of closeness to her. It was so inviting, unlike the museum-like, neutral colors that were throughout the rest of the house. An easel stood near the window and a palette of paints was on the table. She wondered what Jessica's project had been, but didn't ask. Neither said anything about the changes that Jessica had made.

After they had stepped out of the kitchen Clarissa listened until she could hear Sybil and Kenneth talking in the next room. She picked up Kenneth's cell-phone. Knowing that she had time for one quick look, she opened his phone and was about to take a look at his bookmarks when she glanced up and saw Jessica's urn standing on the corner of the countertop. Guiltily she placed his phone back down, got off her chair and walked into the studio.

Kenneth was showing Sybil Jessica's collection of binders, all the ones that she had put together since joining the Blue Marble Club. They were so engrossed in what they were doing that they didn't hear Clarissa enter the room. She almost turned back to look at his phone but instead her eyes were drawn to the canvas on the easel. It was covered with a white sheet. She was tempted to look under the covering for she knew that Jessica hadn't painted anything in years. Maybe she had started something just before she died. But that also didn't make sense for the room was still in shambles and she would never have started a new project with it like that. A palette of paints sat on the little table next to the easel. She shivered, not from cold but because this visit was getting weirder and weirder. The paints looked like they were still wet. She was ready to go, to leave Jessica's house and never to come back.

"Sybil, are you about ready? I should get back home to the kids," Clarissa said.

"How are they Clarissa?" Kenneth asked, hurriedly. "What are their names…now, Cloe and Aiden, isn't it?"

"Yes," she said, giving Sybil another significant look. "They're well."

"Come by anytime," Kenneth said as they left.

Kenneth had hardly closed the door behind them and they weren't even in the car when Clarissa said, "That was way too fucking weird."

"But I'm sure he's not on drugs," Sybil said, seriously.

"Well then he's most certainly off his chump."

"Strangely he seemed to have his wits about him when he was showing me Jessica's books."

"But you heard him; he was talking about Jessica as if she's alive."

"Maybe it was just a slip. They were married for thirteen years and boyfriend-girlfriend for nine before that."

"Yea right, but there were three slips? I'm positive that he's living in denial," Clarissa said.

"I've heard of people doing that. What are the six stages?" Sybil said and began listing them, "Anger, resentment, yearning, suffering, sadness and eventually acceptance?"

"I didn't hear you mention the word denial, in that list. Nor did you mention loony. Well whatever it is, he's creepy. He didn't even ask about Brianna and Simon but he asked about my kids, whom he doesn't even know."

"And what's this about you taking him out on your night to see the owls? Are you changing your tune about him?"

"I don't know what happened there?" she said, shaking her head. "It was almost like I was hypnotised when I was talking to him."

"Like Jessica was?"

"Screw off. You know I can't stand him," Clarissa said, angrily.

"Well something happened in there and truthfully, whatever it was, I'm not sure that I like it," Sybil said, sadly.

CHAPTER FIVE

PETER AND GLORIA, and Brian and Karen, made it a point to visit Kenneth whenever they were in the city. Jeffrey and Christine stopped by even more regularly to check in on him. They were worried that he wasn't taking good care of himself although there wasn't any evidence of weight loss. They would invite him to dinner, which he refused, and aside from going to work every day he spent every hour at home. He seemed to have lost all interest in anything and everything social except for this newfound interest in Jessica's hobby, the Blue Marble Club.

Kenneth now left the front door unlocked, whenever he was home, insisting that when Jeffrey visited, he could just walk in. He said that that made his life easier. Every Thursday evening was their take-away night. That particular evening, Jeffrey and Christine arrived, knocked softly and walked in as Kenneth had insisted. Christine gave Jeffrey *the look*, for she knew that the songs that were playing were the same that Jessica's had played on the night of her suicide. They were also surprised to hear Kenneth talking with someone. Kenneth hadn't entertained at all since Jessica had died. They looked at each other curiously and stepped beyond the foyer.

Kenneth was sitting in the dining room, seemingly entertaining a guest. The lights were low. Jeffrey looked nervously at the bag of take-away then at Christine, thinking that he must have got the day wrong, or Kenneth had forgotten that they were coming.

Christine, never one to hold-back, and nosey to see who his guest was, took another step towards the dining room. Light glistened from the tall, burgundy urn that stood at the opposite end of the table.

Obviously Kenneth hadn't heard their arrival for he continued to speak, "Here's to us my love," as he raised his glass in a toast, "I hope I've laid it out right for you Jessica. I just want to make you happy. Maybe I should sit next to you? I cannot bear to be away from you….. I thought that maybe we could watch a movie tonight? ….I've chosen something for us, one of those soppy love stories. I'll even turn the phone off….. I know how you hate us being disturbed," Kenneth said. Clearly struggling to please her he tilted his head in concentration and listened to the voices inside his head.

Jeffrey and Christine quietly retraced their steps to the door and stepped outside.

"What the hell?" Jeffrey said.

"I thought you said he was doing better. He thinks she's still alive. He's got her fucking urn at the other end of the table."

"He *was* okay. He doesn't act like this at work. He knows it's Thursday and that we would be stopping over tonight."

"What should we do?"

"Hell if I know. I guess, either ring the doorbell or go home," Jeffrey said.

The ringing of the doorbell disturbed Kenneth, "Excuse me my love. I'll only be a minute," he said, getting up to answer the door.

"Oh.... Jeffrey. I had forgotten that you said you were stopping by. Ah yes, the Chinese take-away. Come in," he said, glancing over his shoulder towards the dining room. It was obvious to Jeffrey and Christine that he would rather that they just left.

"If you're busy we could come another time. We can leave the food. Say tomorrow?" Jeffrey asked.

"Nonsense, come on into the kitchen. It's the best place in the house. Jessica's favorite spot."

Christine hesitantly laid out the food and filled their plates. Although they could have sat around the small kitchen table, knowing that the dining room was off-limits, Kenneth and Jeffrey sat at the bar and she stood opposite them. They all leaned against the counter, to eat their dinner.

"You're looking great Kenneth. Why don't you come over to dinner tomorrow evening?" Christine suggested.

"Oh I'm not sure if I can make it to *that*," Kenneth said, glancing over his shoulder, into the dining room. "I kind of thought maybe I'd do up something special myself. After all it is Friday night, you know," raising his eyebrows in an all-knowing way.

The food was hardly eaten when Christine said, looking at her watch, "Holy shit, I totally forgot, I was supposed to phone a client tonight. We really do have to go, Kenneth. Sorry to cut the evening short."

"Hey, it's okay. I understand," Kenneth said, smiling warmly. He was glad that they were leaving for he had made other plans for the night.

Jeffrey and Christine were hardly in the car when they were both talking at once.

"Slow down there Christine."

"But Jeffrey, he thinks that Jessica is still alive."

"Maybe…. but in a harmless way. One would never know it at work. He's the same old Kenneth that he always was."

"And what's that bit about Friday night? What the hell does he think he's doing with her? She's dead."

"I've got a pretty wild imagination but even I can't dream up the answer to that one."

Kenneth returned to the dining room as soon as they left. "I'm sorry Jess, they do mean well," he said, as he sat back down at the head of the table. "Now where were we? Ah yes, a movie, or would you like me to help you with your bath first? It's been ages since I've washed your hair. Oh Jessica, I love you so much. Maybe you're up to having a dance? Your favorite music is playing. I haven't changed the c.d.s. They're exactly the same as the ones that you chose. I've kept everything just as you like it. When you're well again you can choose a new batch."

He smiled, stood and said, "My angel," offering his hand. He danced up and down the foyer to Jessica's favorite songs with her urn in his arms.

He whispered to her, "The children are asking for you. Would you like to go to your beloved Island? I can take you there. But first we have to go and see the Burrowing Owls with Clarissa. She is being so kind."

He paused in his dance, listening.

"Oh yes, she is truly a good friend," he said as he swung her in a wide circle, laughing.

CHAPTER SIX

CLARISSA WAS true to her word and, as promised, had made arrangements for Kenneth to go out to the Burrowing Owls' site for the night. But the closer and closer that the day came for them to spend hours together, inside a hunting blind, alone and in the dark, she became very nervous. As angry as she was at him, blaming him for Jessica's death, she recalled how mesmerized she felt when she talked to him. "You're just being stupid," she said to herself, having discovered that being inside Kenneth's house had increased her feeling of loss of Jessica. But either way, there was no way that she wanted to be alone anywhere with a nut case. And he certainly must be crazy: keeping the house as it was before she died and talking as if she had just stepped out and would be home any moment. Half afraid of him she didn't hesitate to call in the troops. She phoned Sybil.

"Sybil, I'd like you and Nicholas to join me and Kenneth when we go out to the owls' nesting site."

"What? And spend the whole night out there with *him*? Are you fucking joking?" Sybil said, surprising even herself because she rarely swore.

"I'm really nervous about being alone with him. Please….. for Jessica?"

"For Jessica? Don't you start using her too! It's for your sake. You just have to admit it."

"Of course it's for me. I'm feeling nervous about being with him but I'm taking him because Jessica would have loved to get him out there."

"Oh, alright, we'll be there. When?" she said, sighing.

"This Friday, he insisted it be a Friday."

"There he goes with that Friday thing again."

"I'm starting to feel really uncomfortable with this too. Maybe I should have checked his phone. But I couldn't with Jessica right there."

"You're starting to sound like him. Jessica wasn't there. Her ashes were and she's dead," Sybil said, angrily. She hated it that they were fighting on account of Kenneth and she was afraid that he in the end would ruin their friendship. "Maybe we should just steer clear of him entirely?"

"I think you're right. After this, that's it. No more favors," Clarissa said, determined.

****

Kenneth sat on a flat stone, positioning himself on the highest point of that part of the prairie, patiently waiting for Clarissa to arrive at the burrowing owls' location. He watched the sun slip closer and closer to the horizon and marvelled at the sight, for even at this hour the vast sky was uncannily blue. On the opposing horizon an umbrella of tangerine cloud hung over the waning quarter-moon that had just risen. He knew that he had arrived early but he didn't mind waiting almost an hour before Clarissa squeezed her car into the small spot next to his. She saw that there were a dozen other cars there so obviously other members had already set off to their blinds. Clarissa glanced at the cars, searching for Sybil's, but it was not among them.

Kenneth leapt from his rock, swung his back-pack over his shoulder and ambled over to where she had parked.

"I was afraid that I had missed you," he said, smiling.

"Sorry, I stopped to pick up some food and drinks. It might be a long night."

"I didn't even think of that. It takes a woman's touch."

She turned at the sound of a car. "Ah, there they are."

"Who?"

"Sybil and Nicholas."

"Sybil has a new man?" he said, surprised. "I didn't know anyone else was coming."

"I thought it might be more fun as a foursome."

Kenneth's smile disappeared. He shifted his back-pack and shivered when she had said that.

"Are you okay?" she asked. "It gets a bit cool out here at night. I hope you thought to bring a jacket."

"Yea, sure. Yes, I did," he said, distracted.

A series of hugs followed introductions when Sybil and Nicholas joined them.

"Well we best get on," Clarissa said, "We have a three mile hike."

Clarissa and Sybil walked together chatting. Kenneth and Nicholas sauntered along behind making small talk.

"This is my first time out here, how about you?" Kenneth asked.

"My second actually, I came out earlier today to help Clarissa and Sybil set up the blind, I'm not really a nature nut but Sybil wanted me to tag along."

"Did you know that the Burrowing Owls come up here each spring and live in old prairie-dog burrows?"

"The only thing that I know is that they mate for life. Like most birds do I suppose?"

"Like people should," Kenneth said.

Nicholas gave him an odd look before he said, "Isn't it remarkably beautiful out here?"

Kenneth stopped and looked at the prairie, a composition of shrubs, herbs and grasses. The grass was dry and golden in the fading light and there wasn't a tree in sight. "Yes it is." Kenneth said, surprised that he had never noticed that before.

"I think it's a great idea that Clarissa suggested a foursome. It'll make for a more interesting night."

"Please don't use that term," Kenneth said, shifting his back-pack nervously.

They walked in silence for the rest of the way. The hunting blind was not designed for four people, but very soon they managed to arrange themselves in such a way that they could each get a good view out of the narrow slit. They sat in a row with the women in the middle. Kenneth placed his back-pack on his lap. In the darkness he unzipped the top of his bag. They each had a pair of night goggles that they could wear as the time neared. They quietly waited for full darkness, anxious for the owls to crawl out of their burrow, to stretch and take to flight, just as Jessica had seen them do years ago.

At the sight of the first owl Clarissa nudged Sybil and Kenneth. Everyone scrambled for their night goggles. Then all eyes were on the tiny yellow-eyed bird as it stretched its wings and stood as tall as it could. Kenneth raised his back-pack so that the top of Jessica's urn was level with the opening in the tent. Clarissa caught a glint of the light as it reflected from Jessica's urn and, panicking, she stumbled out from the blind. Her disturbance caused the startled bird to race back into the hole.

Sybil was immediately at her side leaving Kenneth and Nicholas inside the tent. She whispered, "What the hell?"

"He's brought Jessica. He has her urn in his bag," Clarissa whispered, as they moved away from the tent.

"You've got to be joking?"

"Sorry, I'm afraid not. He *is* fucking barmy. I knew it. We might as well go home. We won't get any more chances to see another one tonight. Kenneth has fucked that up royally."

They packed up what they had brought and made their walk back to their cars. The narrow yellow beam of Clarissa's flashlight pointed the way. No one said a word except for Sybil who whispered to Clarissa, "Stop over on your way home."

If Kenneth had opened his mouth, or even made a peep of sound, Clarissa would have choked him. Wisely he never said a word. No one gave thought to the tiny owl that had not had the chance of feeding that night.

There were no cheery hugs or greetings when they parted ways in the parking lot.

Sybil and Nicholas were standing in her driveway when Clarissa drove up. She was barely out of her car when she yelled, "See I told you he was bat-shit crazy."

"Shush, you'll have the whole neighborhood out here wondering what's going on. Let's go inside."

Clarissa flopped down onto the sofa next to Sybil while Nicolas poured the drinks.

"Did you see that?" Clarissa asked, "He had Jessica's urn in his bag."

"No, I didn't, actually. Maybe you're wrong."

"No way. Don't try to make me the bad guy here. I know what I saw. I think we should phone

Jeffrey. I need a man's brain. He'll know what to do with Kenneth. They're so alike it makes me sick, yet who else does one call?"

"Ghostbusters?" Sybil said, teasingly. "Why don't we just put this all behind us? Leave Kenneth to do as he pleases. Besides you do realize that it's getting pretty late to phone anyone."

"I don't care. I've had my fill of him."

"And what have I got, if it isn't a man brain?" Nicholas asked.

"Hey, lucky you. You're nothing like *them*," Sybil said, taking his hand in hers.

Jeffrey picked up on the first ring, obviously still awake, "Jeffrey, Clarissa here, Jessica's friend."

"I remember you, very well in fact," Jeffrey said. His hidden meaning was lost on her in her moment of madness and frustration with Kenneth.

"I think you need to talk with Kenneth. He's doing some erratic, stupid things, pretending as if Jessica is still alive."

"I think that he's just spending much too much time alone," he said. "We'll invite him over to dinner. Tomorrow."

CHAPTER SEVEN

JEFFREY KNEW that what Clarissa had said about Kenneth was true. He and Christine had seen it for themselves. Of course he was acting oddly but what can one expect? The man was grieving and Jeffrey hated to imagine how he himself would deal with such a tragedy. In the past weeks they had made numerous invitations for Kenneth to join them for dinner and were faced with equally as many rejections. Jeffrey thought about it long and hard and decided to try a new approach.

At eight o'clock the following morning Jeffrey phoned him. "Kenneth, I'd like you to stop by today if you have the time. Christine and I are thinking of doing some renovations and we would like your opinion." The lie was easy. There were not any renovations in their plans but it might be the only way to get Kenneth in their door. Then once he was there all would be well again and they could slide into the old ways. Jeffrey was certain of that.

"I'm just working a little project myself," Kenneth said, balancing the phone on his shoulder as he placed the palette of paints on the desk and wiped the paint from his hands. "It must be the time of year. It gets everyone into doing things."

"Yes, I suppose so. How about later this afternoon?"

"Yes, that'll work for me."

"Why don't I get Christine to put some dinner together for us? Or is there a rush to get home?"

"Sounds good. No, no rush."

"Perfect. How about four o'clock?" Jeffrey said, hanging up the phone.

He released a long sigh which had Christine saying, "It sounds as though that went well."

"Yes, surprisingly. I'm not sure what Clarissa was going on about. It sounds like he's coming around after all."

"This might make for an interesting night. I might even spice it up a little," she said, laughing.

"I wouldn't expect too much. It's only been four months."

"Like as if you could go without for four months?" she said, laughing.

After he had hung up the phone, Kenneth picked up the palette of paints from the desk with one hand and the paint brush with the other. At the top corner of the canvas he had the photograph of Jessica in the red and white costume that he had dressed her in on their tenth wedding anniversary. He had captured the photograph just as she was beaming him a huge smile. In her hands were two champagne glasses. Her long golden-blonde hair was draped over her left breast covering the exposed nipple. Her right nipple was hard and perky, peeking through the cut-out area of the corset.

Kenneth, no artist, dabbed the brush onto the palette, blended the paints and made another mark on the canvas. However bad the quality of the work was, it left no doubt that he was attempting a portrait of Jessica.

"We'll have to cut today's session short Jessica," he said. "Jeffrey needs a hand. I hope that's okay?"

After a brief pause he added, "Of course I'm taking you with me. I love you," setting the paints down and looking admiringly at his work.

****

Jeffrey had laid out the original blueprints on the coffee-table long before Kenneth arrived. He sat on the sofa, patted the spot next to him for Kenneth to sit on and Christine left the room to get the drinks. Kenneth placed his back-pack between them. They hovered over the blueprints, pointing and discussing the spurious renovation project. Christine opened the beers and, as she had planned, she placed two tiny colored pieces of tissue in Kenneth's beer. 'What's wrong with that,' she thought, 'After all, he wasn't opposed to doing that with Jessica and it's time for him to loosen up a little.' After the little papers had dissolved she served the beer and raised her glass in a toast. "To tomorrow," she said, smiling.

Kenneth slowly sipped his drink as he and Jeffrey continued discussing the moving of walls and planning the changes that would never be made. After a few minutes Kenneth relaxed and leaned back on the sofa, his arm slung over his back-pack. Christine served a snack and before long all thoughts of renovations vanished. Kenneth smiled, relaxing for the first time since Jessica had died.

'This feels great being with friends,' he thought, unaware that he was high on more than just beer.

They later moved to the dining room and Kenneth was sitting in his usual chair. Christine was serving yet another example of her organic food fads: spinach and ricotta pie. He was so relaxed that he had forgotten his back-pack in the living room. He was glad that he had decided to stay for dinner for he hadn't felt this good in months. Kenneth leaned back in his chair and said, "Thanks, Jeffrey, for asking me over."

"Hey, that's what friends are for," he said, raising his glass in a toast.

Christine opened a second bottle of wine and poured. They all smiled.

'This is the perfect start.' Jeffrey thought. 'Maybe next weekend we can make it a night to remember.'

****

Jeffrey started working on Kenneth early in the week, mentioning the renovations again and making yet more false suggestions about improving their house. He felt a bit deceitful in doing that but it was all for Kenneth's own good. He needed to get back into the swing of life. As much as he would have liked to have invited two more couples he knew that it was best to move slowly. In time all would be well again.

Kenneth didn't need a reminder to attend their next dinner and was more than eager to discuss Jeffrey's home improvement plans with him. In fact he had arrived ten minutes early. He placed his backpack on the sofa next to him, Christine poured drinks and Jeffrey spread out the blueprints. Kenneth, unlike during the last visit, was completely relaxed from the outset, leaning back against the sofa. "As for colors," he said, "Jessica is the expert," tapping his back-pack.

"It'll be a few weeks before we have to consider that," Jeffrey said, avoiding any further discussion of Jessica.

Within minutes conversation had changed to office talk, of Marlund, their own company, taking over another small investment firm, Votan Investments.

"We should be able to close this deal in the next two weeks," Jeffrey said.

"And increase our bottom line by another mil at least," said Kenneth.

"Thanks to you."

"Fifty-fifty. It took the both of us to pull it off," Kenneth said, proudly.

"Spoken like a true friend," Jeffrey said, giving Kenneth's shoulder a light squeeze.

"Okay, that's more than enough office talk. Dinner," Christine said, laughing.

Fresh glasses of wine had been placed at each setting. Christine was up to her old tricks and dropped the tiny bits of LSD-soaked paper into Kenneth's glass well before he had sat down. Christine didn't bother to tell Jeffrey that she had hoped for some action from Kenneth that evening, but she was certain that he felt the same way.

Christine made a toast, "To us," she said when Kenneth momentarily realized that he had left his back-pack in the living room. He almost put his glass down and went to get it. Instead he raised his glass and said, "To us."

Kenneth was so relaxed and content that he was hardly aware of what he had eaten. Later when Christine removed the plates from the table and Jeffrey offered him a line of cocaine.

He said, "Why not, what can it hurt."

"My feelings exactly."

When Christine came back into the room she sat next to Kenneth. Although it would have been more comfortable to move back into the living room neither Jeffrey nor Christine mentioned leaving the dining table, because of Kenneth's back-pack sitting dauntingly on the sofa. She lovingly touched his arms and placed her hand on his thigh, slowly moving it higher until she felt his hardness. Jeffrey moved to stand behind Kenneth and placed his hand over his breast, stroking his nipple. Kenneth moaned. Christine squirmed, rubbing her hard nipples against his arm, anxious to have Kenneth's helmet-headed warrior inside her shame cave, as she had referred to it when they went to Las Vegas together. Jeffrey's cock twitched.

    Within minutes Jeffrey and Christine were removing his clothes, one piece at a time. Christine kissed Kenneth's lips and Jeffrey slid his mouth back and forth over Kenneth's cock. It had been a long time since they were together like this and it was hard for them to slow the pace. Christine threw a blanket on the floor in the foyer and their three bodies intertwined as one. None of them noticed the light that glinted from the long, slender, burgundy urn that stuck out from the top of Kenneth's back-pack in the living room. They were simply too crazily mad for sex to give it any thought.

CHAPTER EIGHT

JEFFREY WALKED into Kenneth's office and said, "How about a round of golf? That Votan deal closed today and I think it's time to celebrate."

Kenneth looked at the calendar. "It closed early. I thought it was closing next week," he said, surprised. With hardly a second's thought he added, "Hey, why not? I haven't been out for ages."

Jeffrey smiled. Last weekend seemed to have put Kenneth back in good form. All will be *good to go* from here on in. Now might be the perfect day to discuss their next Callisto Akantha get-away.

Sweat rolled down Kenneth's back as he pulled his golf clubs from the car. He said to Jeffrey, smiling, "Hottest day for years, they say."

"Might as well get used to it…. Climate change."

"So they say. I've been reading Jessica's books and I've just started the one on the Northern Leopard Frog. You do know of the Blue Marble Club?"

"Yes. I do..." Jeffrey said and anxious to move all conversation away from Jessica he added, "Hey is that George Farquarson throwing his clubs in the car?"

"You're right, it is. Well I'll be darned. I haven't seen him in ages. I thought he was dead"

"Let's see if he wants to have a beer. We have plenty of time before tee-time."

After drinking a couple of beers Kenneth relaxed completely. It was just like old times as they laughed and shared tales.

"Okay, tee time," Jeffrey said.

"Already? Hey it was great seeing you again George. We'll have to keep in touch," Kenneth said, without enthusiasm, as they got up to leave.

Jeffrey was glad that George hadn't mentioned Jessica.

They were just starting the second hole when Jeffrey said, "Christine and I are going to another of Callisto Akantha's retreats. Care to join us?"

"Oh.... I'm not so sure about that place."

"There are great views of Lake McDonald and Heaven's Peak up there."

"I don't know. I'm trying to put all that stuff behind me."

"How about I put you down and you can think about it?"

"And relinquish my deposit?"

"Don't worry. I'll cover for you if you change your mind." Jeffrey said this very off-handily though he would be really pissed off if he were to lose the money.

"If it pleases you, you can put me down, but I don't think I'll be going."

"The chalets go quickly in our group. I think I'll risk it and pay your way," Jeffrey said.

Kenneth lined up his club and made a good three hundred yard shot.

"Looks like you have your game-face on. Or is it Callisto Akantha that's done it for you?"

"Who knows? Maybe both," Kenneth said, teasingly.

When Kenneth returned to his car he was surprised to see that he had forgotten his back-pack on the front seat. He hadn't once thought about it or Jessica, not while they had their drinks in the clubhouse or through the whole of the game. The top of the urn was just barely sticking out the zipper of his bag. He touched it and it was hot from the sun. It burned his fingertips. Startled, he gave it a questioning look. It seemed to him that Jessica was reminding him of her presence and punishing him.

****

Kenneth didn't return to work. When he got home he placed Jessica's urn on the desk in his old office, next to her collection of books from the Blue Marble Club. He had seen a frog on the golf course that afternoon and he wondered if it was the Northern

Leopard Frog. What else could it have been with all those spots? He pulled out the binder and sure enough on the front cover was a glossy picture of the same frog. There was no doubt. He read through every page absorbing every bit of information that he could. At two o'clock in the morning he realized that he hadn't even stopped for dinner. Too tired to bother he simply climbed the stairs, with Jessica's urn under his arm, and went directly to the guest bedroom and slept.

Nor did he go in to work the following day. Instead he turned on his computer and learned even more about the Northern Leopard Frog, making additional notes of his own. By mid-afternoon he was so excited about that little amphibian that his interest in joining the Blue Marble Club was renewed.

Kenneth phoned Clarissa, "I've just been reading up on the Leopard Frog, Clarissa, and I'm even more serious about joining the Club."

"Kenneth, I hate to tell you this but you can't join just because this was Jessica's passion."

"Clarissa, you don't know me at all. I want to do this for me, for us, for the world. I'm taking Jessica's books and I'm going out today to look for the frogs."

"You're doing what?"

"Come with me and you'll see. In order to save this frog one really has to understand it."

There was a pause on the other end of the phone.

Kenneth added, "You don't believe me do you?"

"Of course I do. Why wouldn't I?" She lied, suspecting full well that he was slipping ever further over the edge into insanity.

"Then join me. This is for Jessica."

'Why did you have to say that?' she thought, remembering that she too had used the same line on Sybil. "Alright," she said, unwillingly.

"Say seven o'clock at Allen Bill Pond. That'll give us a few hours before sunset."

Clarissa hung up the phone and thought about Kenneth's phone call. There was absolutely no doubt that he had been acting way too weirdly since Jessica had died. And here she was forced into doing what *he* wanted. She wondered if this was the side of Kenneth that Jessica had not been able to say no to. "Well, you can rest assured that I won't get sucked into any of his antics," she said aloud, turning away from the phone.

Throughout the day Clarissa repeatedly looked at the time. She kept reminding herself that she wasn't anxious to meet up with Kenneth. This whole situation was making her anxious. Before she left she took out a cooler and threw in some crackers and cheese. She added a bottle of wine and two glasses. 'Might as well be comfy if we have to sit out under the stars looking at those fucking frogs,' she thought, trying to justify her actions. She arrived at their rendezvous location a full twenty minutes ahead of Kenneth, but she didn't mind as the weather was warm and it was a beautiful spot. She parked her car on the side road, took the cooler from the back seat, walked to the south end of the pond and sat on one of the enormous flat rocks. It was so tranquil with the birds singing and the sun warm against her face that she felt lost in time. She was smiling when Kenneth placed his back-pack down and sat beside her.

"You have a beautiful smile," he said.

"Oh come on. You've known me for years and you've never said that before," she said blushing.

"I'm sorry to say that I've never noticed it before. I'm seeing things quite differently this past while."

'Yes, since Jessica died,' Clarissa thought, but instead she said, "It must be the nature that draws it out. It is quite lovely here."

They sat in silence listening to the sounds around them. There was the occasional croak from a frog. As the sun edged ever closer to the craggy peaks of the Rocky Mountains in the distance it cast a long shadow along the hills. Clarissa said, in a whisper and almost to herself, "I miss Jessica so much."

Kenneth said nothing. He either didn't hear her or he pretended not to hear. In the fading light he whispered, pointing, "Look, over there, a leopard frog." He unzipped his backpack and took out his camera. Neither said a word as Kenneth snapped the picture.

"Calls for a celebration," she said, taking out the cheese, crackers and wine.

"I didn't even think to bring anything," he said, taking her hand in his and stroking his thumb across the back of her hand.

She looked into his eyes and pulled away. She was so close to kissing him. It seemed perverse, 'What the hell am I thinking?' she thought to herself. 'What kind of a person am I, my husband at home with my kids and here I am being smitten by my best friend's widower? And he's a louse too.'

She hastily opened the crackers and set the cheese out. As much as she needed a drink right then she felt uncertain if she should even open it, fearful that she would become too relaxed. She need not have bothered hesitating for Kenneth uncorked the wine and poured two glasses.

It was almost midnight when they drove back into the city. The last thing that Clarissa said to Kenneth before leaving the pond was, "Okay, I'll recommend you as a member of the Blue Marble Club. When I get the application I'll bring it over."

CHAPTER NINE

THE FOLLOWING morning Clarissa phoned Sybil. "Can we meet for coffee? We need to talk."

"Of course, the usual spot?"

Minutes later Clarissa was sitting across from Sybil at The Office. A warm breeze and bird song wafted through the open windows. In the light of a new day Clarissa's encounter last evening with Kenneth seemed less disturbing. Clarissa wrapped her hands around her coffee cup and looked at Sybil. Their friendship was strong and she knew that she could confide anything in her.

"I think I almost kissed Kenneth last night," Clarissa blurted out before even taking a sip of her coffee.

"You did what? In your dreams you mean? I've been having nightmares too since Jessica died," Sybil said, shaking off a shiver.

"No, for real. Last night I almost kissed Kenneth. I don't know what happened."

"Oh, come on! You don't know what happened? And what were you doing with him at night anyway?"

"We were at Allen Bill Pond looking at leopard frogs?"

"Frogs, oh come on. That's a pretty weak excuse. It's not like you're twelve."

"But it was almost as if I was mesmerized. I looked into his eyes and….."

"You looked into his eyes? What the hell for? What did you think you'd see?"

"I don't know… I don't remember."

"Well maybe you ought to remember that he is Jessica's husband."

"Was Jessica's husband. You sound like Kenneth talking about her as if she's still alive." Clarissa said, then started to cry. "What the hell is the matter with me? Jerry and I have a good marriage. I have two beautiful children and a good husband."

Sybil looked at her, disgusted, when she asked, "Did you fuck him?" surprising even herself at such a question.

"Of course not."

"Then why does it sound like you're already divorcing Jerry?"

"I didn't even kiss him. I thought, if anyone, that you'd understand. Maybe I was wrong," Clarissa said, crying and getting up to leave.

"Please don't go. I'm sorry."

"I'm sorry too. I don't know why but I feel so confused. I would never divorce Jerry. We have a great life together and I love him to bits, but…."

"But……what?"

"I don't know. I have butterflies just thinking about that moment."

"If it's just butterflies then go out and buy a can of fucking *Raid* and kill it before it spreads. Whatever you're trying not to say does not sound good."

Clarissa said defensively, "I'm not, not trying to say anything."

"You're saying a whole lot more than you think."

They were still both upset when Clarissa left but neither saw any point in sitting together. For ten minutes they sat across from each other in silence, wondering what the other was thinking.

Sybil was so mad at her that she didn't even bother telling her that she and Nicholas were going to PEI the following week.

****

A few days later Kenneth phoned Clarissa, "I was thinking about uploading those pictures that we took the other day at Allen Bill Pond. I thought it only fair that you were here for that."

"Why don't you just email me a copy of them?"

"There must be at least fifty. Come on, let's do it together."

"Fifty? Then just pick out the best ones and send them to me," she said, nervous about being alone with him.

"That would be pointless now wouldn't it? After all it was *our* little project."

She wondered where that came from and thought, 'That's news to me. Our little project?' Knowing that there was no way of winning an argument with him she said, reluctantly, "Alright, when?"

"Right now if that works for you."

Clarissa looked at the time and said, sighing, "Okay, I'll be right over." She still had three hours before she had to think about dinner.

They sat side by side at Jessica's grandfather's old desk, in the room that Jessica had been going to use as a studio. Clarissa glanced around the room and she fixed her eyes on the canvas that was still sitting on the easel under a sheet. She eyed it curiously, wondering again what was under the cover, then glanced at Kenneth who was concentrating on transferring the pictures. She was absolutely certain that Jessica hadn't started painting again before her suicide. Sybil and Clarissa would have been the first to know. It bothered her that she didn't know what was happening in Jessica's house. It was as if walls had suddenly been erected, only allowing information to trickle to her and Sue. Not that there was much trickling happening because she felt totally out of the loop. She felt very confused.

"There. All done," Kenneth said, pleased. "Let's take a look. But first a glass of wine."

He came back into the room, handed her a glass and tipped his glass in a toast. "To frogging," he said,

She smiled, hesitantly, before raising her glass as well.

One by one they clicked through the pictures. Each picture offered little difference from the previous one. Kenneth was right, there were at least fifty shots, and after a while their little oohs and aahs for the leopard spotted frogs stopped. Kenneth had his hand on her leg and he was stroking it up and down. From time to time he would rest it near her crotch and give her a gentle squeeze. She squirmed. When there was an exceptionally good photo he clutched her hand and leaned his head against hers, pleased with the photos. She was surprised when he placed a kiss on her hand, then her cheek, then her lips and she shocked herself by kissing him back. Her heart was racing and he stirred emotions in her that she never knew that she had. At that moment Clarissa wanted so badly to have sex with Kenneth. She fidgeted in her chair, spreading her legs and releasing a long low moan. Suddenly they reached the last of the frog pictures and the next picture was one of Jessica in her tenth anniversary costume. Clarissa gasped and looked directly at Kenneth.

"That is most certainly one of Jessica's best," he said, proudly.

Clarissa was speechless. She stumbled to her feet and accidentally pulled the sheet from the painting. It was similar to the one of Jessica in the photograph on Kenneth's computer screen, but the painting was of very poor quality. 'Who the hell is painting that?' she wondered. But in her heart she knew. She suddenly wondered where Kenneth had placed Jessica's urn. On every other occasion it had been next to them, but not that time.

Clarissa grabbed her purse and murmured an excuse to leave. She was so angry with herself. Deep inside she felt a deep ache that was new to her. It was an ache that she knew that only he, Jessica's Kenneth, could cure. After Sybil's insults last week when she told her how she had *almost* kissed Kenneth, she knew that there was no way that she could talk to her about this. Clarissa drove directly to Sue's house. The whole way there, all she could think of was Kenneth and having his cock inside her. She felt terrible. She felt as if she was betraying Jessica, her best friend, totally forgetting any loyalty that she should hold to her own husband, Jerry, and to her friends, Sue and Sybil.

In her heart she knew that those thoughts made her unfaithful to Jessica's memory. But strangely she didn't feel at all guilty about *almost* cheating on Jerry. In fact in all her fifteen years of marriage she had never even thought of cheating on him, until now. And the reward seemed well worth the deceit.

"Sorry for just stopping over but….."
"What is it?" Sue asked, seeing Clarissa's flushed face. "Are you okay?"
"Yes…. no…. oh I don't know."
"Come and sit," she said, leading her to the sofa.
"I did something really bad."

"Come on, I know you better than that. How bad could it be?"

"I kissed Kenneth," she blurted it out.

"You did what?"

"You heard me….. I don't know what to do."

"Don't move. I'll get us a drink."

Clarissa was picking at her fingers when Sue returned.

"Okay, from the top," Sue said.

"I guess it started a few days ago when he asked me to join him at Allen Bill Pond to see the Northern Leopard Frogs. Can you believe that? We had a few drinks, waited for the frogs and took some pictures."

"Pretty unusual way of doing a nature walk. What then?"

"Well, I almost kissed him that night. It was so romantic out at the pond with the frogs croaking. Then that was it, we went home."

"Each to your own home I hope. Clarissa what were you thinking?"

"Of course my own home, what do you take me for, some easy slut? You sound like Sybil?"

"And the kiss?"

"I didn't do it. Not then anyway."

"So…. when did you kiss him?"

"Today. A half hour ago. But not on the lips, just on his cheek. "

"You've got to be kidding me. You kissed the wolf in sheep's clothing. Did you forget that Jessica is dead on account of him? The three of us have talked about it enough and we all know that he is manipulative, calculating and deceitful."

"I know….but…."

"But what?"

"It was nice, the way he touched me."

"Nice? He touched you?" she said with distain.

"Yes, but not the way you think. I think I now understand how Jessica got caught. He is charming, almost hypnotising, and a romantic. I couldn't help myself."

"Couldn't help yourself!" Sue said with a sneer. "You sound as though you're a teenager."

"That's what Sybil said to me the other day. I'm not….. and we're supposed to be friends."

"Well, do friends kiss their best friend's widower? And what about Jerry? Your *husband*, Jerry?"

"What do you mean? I didn't really do anything wrong. It was only a caring kiss."

"They have a yard stick for measuring caring? Just be sure that you don't let your caring go too far."

Both Clarissa and Sue were upset when she left but there was nothing more to say. Sue's warning kept ringing in her ears.

CHAPTER TEN

BRIANNA AND SIMON were pleased when their Nana Janet took them to the same school that they had attended before and enrolled them again for the following school term. In her own mind Janet knew that if she didn't take care of that right away neither they nor she would enjoy the summer vacation.

Brianna skipped all the way to the car, clutching her Grandmother's hand. As they left the school she was singing a little ditty. Simon, being his usual rambunctious self, was running circles around the two of them.

"Can we go down to the cottage this summer, Nana?" Simon asked, saying the word *down* when it was actually up on the north shore. Saying it the maritime way.

"We'll have to talk to gramps and see if he has it ready."

"I can help, I'm almost eight."

"We'll see. And speaking of birthdays, we'll have to start planning your party now won't we."

"I want to go to the singing beach, just like mama used to do when she was little like me."

"I'm sure that we can do that. And what about you Brianna, what would you like to do?"

"I'd like to go tobogganing and sleigh riding."

"Then we have to hope for early snowfall. It's nice to make plans isn't it? Now into the car with you," she said, laughing.

The children sang their favorite songs all the way home. All their gaiety assured Janet that she had made the right decision in registering them early for school.

****

There was a stranger's car in the drive when they got home. Janet nervously got out of the car and within seconds had a child's hand firmly gripped in each of her own. The children looked up at her tightly pursed lips and wondered what could be so frightful. As they walked past the car Janet read the rental car agency sticker and gripped their hands even tighter. When Alicia stepped out of the house and onto the porch Janet's grip relaxed.

"Oh Alicia, how nice to see you. I didn't know you were coming," Janet said, releasing the children's hands, practically running and opening her arms to give Alicia a hug.

"Thank you Janet. I wasn't sure……"

"Nonsense. Come in. I'll put the tea on. I hope you're planning to stay." She turned back to Brianna and Simon and said, "Come on children, we have company."

"I don't want to impose," said Alicia.

"Of course not. We would love to have you. Brianna and Simon come and meet Alicia, your mother's old friend."

Brianna bounded towards Alicia and offered her hand in introduction. She said, "I'm Brianna and I'm ten."

"I'm Alicia and I'm very pleased to meet you Brianna. What a lovely name," she said, taking her hand. There was that same soft touch that Jessica had had.

"I like yours too," she said, smiling.

Janet edged Simon forward, "And Simon," she said.

Alicia crouched down and took his hand in hers. "My pleasure," she said, giving him a reassuring squeeze.

"Would you like to see my dolls?" Brianna asked.

"I'd love to," she said, looking questioningly at Janet.

At Janet's nod she followed Brianna to her room. Alicia remembered the room from her last visit. It was Jessica old room and little was changed since she was last there. Within minutes they were both sitting on the floor with a wide collection of dolls completing the circle around them.

At the gentle knock on the door Brianna jumped up and said to Alicia, "Nana always brings tea for my dolls. It's our doll party."

She entered carrying a tray filled with miniature tea cups, tea, cookies and cakes. Brianna carefully placed one in front of each of them and the dolls, naming each doll as she did so, poured the tea and placed the tray in the center.

It was a tea party unlike any that Alicia had attended before. Janet interrupted Brianna's fantasy world by saying, "Okay. Time to settle Alicia into her room. I've got supper to prepare."

After the dishes were cleared away and the children were settled for the night Grandfather James offered Alicia a beer.

"Care for one?" he asked. "I brewed it myself. I try to run off two batches a year. Any more than that and I'd have more than I could drink," he said, chuckling.

"Thanks, I'd like that."

"We're glad you came over," Janet said, with half a smile.

"I'm sorry. It was selfish really to come. I just needed to……"

"It's been hard for all of us."

"I loved her so much," Alicia said, crying.

"I know. We know. We saw it then," Janet said, getting up and wrapping her arms around Alicia.

"We had coffee on *that* afternoon," Alicia said, feeling that she had to explain every last minute of Jessica's life. "I knew that something was wrong but I had no idea."

"None of us did really. Though we knew something was not right."

"Jessica would be happy that the children are here."

"I hope so."

"She really loved it here. She hated living in Alberta and always talked of when they would move back."

"Kenneth promised her that?" Janet asked, surprised. "Hah, I cannot imagine that that would ever have happened. He liked having her to himself."

"He did like to have control of her." She paused then said, "I'm sorry. I'm talking out of turn."

"Nonsense, you haven't said more than we already knew."

"I was planning to stay on the island for a week, but I can't impose. There are dozens of B and Bs."

"Impose? Of course not. What kind of folks would we be if we allowed you to go live next door? You are Jessica's friend and are always welcome in our home."

Alicia hardly took a step without Brianna at her side and by the end of the week they were hard and fast friends. Brianna clung to her as she said her goodbyes. Alicia's promise to visit again was not just for Brianna's sake but for own as well. She tried to hide her tears.

****

Sybil and Nicholas arrived in Charlottetown on the same day that Alicia left. Not that they would have known each other, even if they had rubbed shoulders. It was the usual family homecoming that had Janet, James, Brianna and Simon at the airport to welcome them.

Sybil clung to the children as if they were her own and cried, though at least a dozen times on the flight she had promised Nicholas that she wouldn't. She told him that it was her responsibility as an adult to remain strong for the kids.

They piled into the SUV. Sybil sat next to Brianna and said, "Okay, the first thing that we have to do is get you registered for golfing lessons. Your mother wanted that for you…. And you, you little jigger, what is your fancy?" she asked Simon.

"I want to play hockey like Wayne Gretsky."

"I would have thought you'd choose a more recent star player, like Sidney Crosby since he's a lot closer to home. He's from Nova Scotia."

"No, Gretsky's the best and I'd like to be just like him. He played for the Oilers you know."

Sybil didn't like the idea of Simon playing such a dangerous sport and she said, "Are you sure? They get pretty rough playing hockey?"

"Sure, that's what I want," Simon said, laughing.

How could she possibly say no to that?

"I got a new friend: mommy's friend, Alicia," Brianna said. "She visited me. I want her to move here."

"Really?" Sybil said, giving Janet a questioning look.

"Yup, she is real nice."

"She's my friend too," Simon said, not wanting to be left out.

"Of course she is," Janet said, settling any questions in that regard.

The moment that Sybil was alone with Janet, she said, "So mom, who's this Alicia that the kids are so crazy about?"

"Jessica's friend."

"From where?"

"Calgary, don't you know her?"

"No, I don't. I'm surprised that Jessica never mentioned her."

"She came here when Jessica was here, last year."

"Really? Why?"

"You figure it out. I'm not one to point fingers or judge."

"You're joking, right?"

"All I know is what I saw. She was a whole lot better for Jessica than Kenneth ever was. They loved each other dearly."

"My God. I never would have known. I wonder why we never heard about her?"

"It doesn't matter. She is really good for the children and Jessie would have wanted it this way. She is so kind and gentle. I love her too. So enough of that. Let's tuck those darlings in and let's have one of papa's beers." She ended their talk, recalling how Jessica would hold Alicia's hand and look so lovingly into her face. She wished then that Jessica and Alicia had stayed on the Island. No one would have questioned their love for each other. 'If only…. if only' she thought with a sigh.

Sybil and Nicholas combed the beaches for shells, like children, while Brianna and Simon dawdled along behind. This was her first trip home since Jessica had died. She showed him where she and Jessica used to swim. They walked along the high, red sandstone cliffs and let the warm Atlantic breeze blow through their hair. As the days slipped past she was reminded that they had to go back to Alberta and it made her sad. She would never have gone west if not for Jessica, and suddenly it seemed that there was nothing to go back for, except Nicholas. But he was sitting next to her and not out west. Maybe she could convince him to stay? But first he had to see the Island through her eyes. He must learn to appreciate the richness of the red soil, the fields of wheat waving in the wind, the corn stalks as they stood so proudly…. and the ever present restless sea.

But she dared not even ask, even though they had been practically living together ever since that dreadful night when Jessica took her own life. He hadn't even proposed. She didn't want to be too presumptuous, so she said nothing. But going back to Calgary was going to be harder than ever after these two weeks on the Island.

Nicholas read the classified ads every morning. Maybe, just maybe, there was a chance that there was an opening at a brokerage in Charlottetown. He surfed the internet. He tried to picture himself as an Islander. He liked the look of what he saw. But it was too soon to mention it.

James, on the other hand, knew what Nicholas was about as he carefully rolled the newspaper for the fire when Nicholas was done with it, removing all evidence of his covert searches. He liked sharing their unspoken secret and smiled.

Yes, life in the O'Malley household was as good as it could be… until they thought about Jessica.

CHAPTER ELEVEN

TWO WEEKS following their evening of leopard-frog watching, Kenneth phoned Clarissa again. "I was wondering if you got that application form for my membership in the Blue Marble Club?" he asked.

"Yes, actually it just came in yesterday," she said, though she had received it days before. As much as she had wanted to rush it over to him on that same day, she hadn't.

"You want me to stop over to pick it up?" he asked.

"There's a section that I must fill out so maybe it would be better if I came over to your house?" she said. And immediately asked herself, 'What the hell did I say that for?' filled with a desire to be with him again.

"Okay. That's a good idea. I wanted to talk to you about the decline in the bee population as well. I've been reading a lot about that recently. It's terrible."

"I could bring my books also. When should I come by?" Clarissa asked, hoping that he would ask her over right now. Even though she knew that there was a good possibility that she was getting in deeper than she could handle, she couldn't stop herself.

"I'd like that Clarissa. Say three o'clock?"

"Perfect," she said, releasing a huge sigh.

From the moment that Clarissa heard Kenneth's voice on the other end of the phone her heart was racing. She tried convincing herself that it was nothing, but there was no denying her shaking hand as she put the phone down. She momentarily wondered if she should phone him back to cancel. It would certainly be a whole lot more sensible if he were to stop over at her place, where her kids were running about and Jerry was sitting in his recliner chair, switching channels on the television. She surprised herself when she looked across the room at Jerry and for the first time thought about how dull their lives had become.

She hardly recognized her own voice when she yelled angrily at the kids, "Stop your running. This isn't a race track," hastily going upstairs to change clothes. Maybe Jessica's death was causing her to lose her grip? There were so many things that seemed out of sorts.

She changed into a sundress and swept her hair off her face. She looked into the full-length mirror and ran her hands down her body, turning from left to right. She smiled at her reflection. Even she had to admit that she looked pretty good for a woman of thirty five who had gone through two pregnancies. Her weight was a bit over the average but she carried it well. She never had the model figure that Jessica had but she would always justify it by saying it gave her more of a womanly shape.

On her way out the door she grabbed her binder about the bees, and the application form, and yelled, "Not sure when I'll be back."

Cloe and Aiden answered her, "Okay Mom." Jerry didn't even look up from the football game. He simply grunted. Clarissa closed the door, sighed, and had forgotten all about them by the time she was in her car. As she turned the ignition her thoughts immediately switched to Kenneth. She glanced at the membership form again knowing that if not for her influence Kenneth would never have qualified as a member of the Blue Marble Club.

Too many people had, in the past, signed up, with good intentions and their memberships ended up being more bother than they were worth. Since then the rules had changed and now memberships were only allowed if an existing member were to sponsor the new applicant. She reminded herself that she was doing this for Jessica, yet Clarissa was really impressed by Kenneth's seriousness and she felt that he could actually make a positive difference. With Kenneth's money and influential associates maybe, just maybe, they could move towards a cleaner province. Perhaps the voices of the Blue Marble Club would eventually be heard.

Clarissa rang the doorbell five times before Kenneth answered it. He swept the door open widely with a bow, "Sorry, I was out on the patio.... Welcome madam," he said, sweeping her into his arms. Music played through the sound system. Clarissa didn't know that it was one of the five c.d.s that Jessica had selected for the dinner party; the dinner party that she had never planned to attend.

Clarissa clung to him. It felt good to be held in that way and they swayed to the music. She momentarily thought of Jerry, sitting in front of the television, and she wondered what had happened to the joie de vivre that was once in their marriage. "Oh my goodness, that's quite a welcome," she said, laughing.

"It's a very small way of showing my appreciation for all that you've done. I'm well aware that if not for you I would never have been able to become a member of the club. Come and see what I've discovered today," he said, as he took her hand and led her out onto the patio.

She was surprised to see that he had laid out a late lunch and a bottle of white wine was chilling. He sat her in a chair and placed a book in her hand.

"It's the whooping crane," he said, "Listen to this," turning on his tablet and playing the single bugle-like notes. He let the notes play on for a full minute. "That is so romantic," he said. Then pointing to the book, "And look at those elegant lines. They are so graceful." His other hand slid up and down her arm and it grazed her breast.

She shivered in spite of the afternoon heat and her nipples hardened. She stood, "I really should go. You can fill out the form and I can come by to pick it up another day."

"Go? But you can't go. Let's have lunch. And I wanted to discuss the whooping crane... We need to help save it," he said, placing both hands on her shoulders and steering her back into the chair. "Did you know that there are fossils of the whooping crane that date back three and a half million years?"

Kenneth's enthusiasm amused her. She suddenly felt as if she had been swept into another world, another life, maybe another love.

"No, I didn't. But what about the bees?" she asked, spellbound and laughing as he placed a kiss on her lips. Unable to stop herself she stood and wrapped her arms around him. They held each other. Kenneth closed his eyes, kissed her again and she kissed him back. It was a long lingering kiss that only two people who have lived and loved could share. Kenneth pressed his hand against her back and she moulded her body to his. "Ahhhh," Clarissa sighed. It felt so good.

He gently pulled away and placed his finger under her chin, "That too, all of it. Now for lunch," he said, sitting her back in her chair and placing a tender kiss on her forehead.

Clarissa was breathless as Kenneth put a glass of wine in her hand. He pulled a chair next to hers and removed the covers from the food. She wondered who had prepared this elegant lunch for she had never seen Kenneth make anything more than Kraft Dinner before. He took a morsel of food and placed it in her mouth. They shared the lunch, she fed him and he fed her, and they both drank the wine. They talked for hours about what they could do to protect the endangered species of Alberta and neither realized that the day was getting on.

Clarissa leaned back in her chair; completely besotted, when Kenneth stepped inside the house. The music stopped and began playing again. Kenneth returned with a second bottle, and said, "New c.d. I bought it on impulse."

"It's nice. I like it," Clarissa said, not knowing that he had removed Jessica's c.d. collection from the player for the new one.

He poured more wine and he asked her to dance. He swept her into his arms and waltzed her around the deck. She nuzzled against his neck and he held her closely. He slid his hand along her spine and he edged the hem of her dress over her thigh. She kissed him passionately and slid her pussy along his leg. He led her to an Adirondack chair, another piece of furniture that Jessica had brought from PEI to Alberta. Neither gave thought to Jessica, nor cared.

Kenneth sat in the chair and leaned against the sloped back. He was dashingly good looking, even more handsome than Clarissa had ever noticed before. He clung to her hand guiding her to sit on his lap and he threw his head back with his eyes closed. She hiked her skirt over her thighs and straddled him. She could feel his hard penis against her pussy. She spread her legs even wider, panted and ground against him, drawing the neckline of her dress under her breasts, freeing them. Kenneth licked her breasts and suckled them as a child would a mother. He unzipped his pants, releasing his cock and he slipped his fingers inside her panties. She was hot and moist. Without removing her panties he guided his penis inside her hot silky pussy. She rode him slowly, her breasts rising and falling with her every stroke. The friction of his cock inside her was unbearably blissful. Her head was thrown back in complete ecstasy. Kenneth had both hands on her hips; grasping, clutching and directing her body over his shaft. Even in the late afternoon air sweat rolled down her back as she took long, slow strokes. It was absolute heaven and she wanted those moments to last forever. They climaxed together and neither thought about nor considered how this event might affect the rest of their lives.

****

Sybil phoned Sue. "We need to talk," she said.
"Sure, anytime. Your place or mine."
"I don't care but I have the most horrible feeling about something."
"Come on over. Is Clarissa coming?"
"More like, has Clarissa come?"
"Lord, I can't believe you said that. And why so cryptic?'
"You might as well crack open the hard stuff. I'll be there in ten."

Sybil turned off the ignition and swung the car door open at the same time as she got out. She practically ran up the walkway. Sue had the door open and held a glass of scotch in her hand.

"Here you go. It sounded as though you needed one really badly."

"You know me as well as I know myself. Thanks," Sybil said, talking a large gulp.

"What's up? I've never seen you so anxious before."

"This is more than anxious. When was the last time that you saw Clarissa?" she asked before she even sat down.

"Oh, I don't know? Three or four weeks ago, I guess," Sue said, thoughtfully.

"Me too. This is totally unlike her. Ever since we met we have visited each other at least two or three times a week. The longest that we've ever been apart is when either of us was on vacation. And she sure as hell hasn't left town."

"Okay, spit it out. What do you know that I don't?"

"That's the trouble... I don't know anything for sure. But I do know what intuition tells me."

"And what might that be."

"He's fucking her," Sybil said, putting her hand over her mouth. "Oh my God, ever since Jessica died my mouth has turned into a bloody sewer."

"I know. It's been hard on all of us. So who's screwing who?"

"Kenneth and Clarissa. I can just see it now, Kenneth sticking his hard cock to her."

"Oh my God, why would you say such a thing?" Sue asked, astonished.

"Just give it one good guess. Phone her house and I'll bet you she's not there. Phone her store and she'll have that girl in working for her. Then try her cell phone and she won't answer that either. The only time that she *never* answers her cell phone is when she's having sex. And we both know that she and Jerry never get it on very much. You do know what I mean?"

"Maybe she's taking flying lessons or art lessons. She always did say that she wanted to do both," Sue said, trying to stick up for Clarissa. She felt like they were ganging up on her and she wasn't there to defend herself.

"Maybe I'm losing my mind…. And, speaking of art lessons, I forgot to tell you that there was a canvas on the easel in Jessica's studio. I know for a fact that she didn't start painting again. She didn't even have the room ready."

"Finish your drink and I'll get you another… You're a wreck."

"Maybe you're right, but where is she?"

"I don't know. Death does strange things to people. Maybe it hurts her too much to hang around with us? Maybe this is her grieving time?"

"Maybe she's with Kenneth? She did say that he mesmerized her, like he did Jessica." Sybil said it mockingly. "That was the exact term that she used. And she told me that she almost kissed him."

"Well, she actually did kiss him," Sue said. "But only on the cheek, a caring kiss, she told me. Go easy on her, we're all hurting."

"Well she'd better watch out about how much she cares. I was fooled by his charming self." She paused and thought about what she had just said and realized that she had no basis for it. "Now I feel like a real shit talking about her as if she has betrayed us and Jessica. I don't even know if she really has. Maybe she really is taking golfing lessons. Who knows? You're probably right, she just needs time."

"Yes Sybil, like we all do. Remember it takes a year to get through the worst of it but even then life will never be the same."

"Cheers anyway, here's to us," Sybil said, tipping her glass. "I wish Clarissa and Jessica were here and everything was like it used to be."

"Don't we all?"

CHAPTER TWELVE

SYBIL'S INTUITION was absolutely spot on, for Clarissa could not get enough of Kenneth. Sue gave thought to Sybil's suspicions and momentarily wondered if she should act on it that very day. And if Clarissa had had an inkling about what Sybil suspected, she herself might have ended it then and there. Embarrassment might have been enough of a driving force for her to see reality. But since she had managed to keep it a secret, it went on.

She laughingly remembered how defensive she had felt when Sybil and Sue reminded her that she was not a teenager. No, she certainly wasn't but she felt like she was sixteen again and in love for the first time. Her body tingled with the sensations that one could only experience at one's very first love-making. After that first time, when they had first made love in the fading light out on the patio, she spent more time at Kenneth's house than at her own. He had stirred a desire in her that she forgotten. He filled her with a yearning to have sex with him forever and always. He made her feel so horny that when she was not with him all she thought about was sex. She would do anything to have sex with Kenneth. And she would do anything that he asked of her in order to get it.

Because of her new-found passion she was more and more often questioning what was left of her relationship with Jerry, if anything at all. She knew in her heart that Jerry had *never* made her feel the way that Kenneth did. She knew the signs of love: the quickening of her sensory organs, her fingertips becoming more sensitive, her hearing more acute and her vision exquisitely precise. Yes, Clarissa was in love with Kenneth and he was her first *true* love.

Clarissa tried to justify her feelings and asked herself every day, 'And what is the matter with that anyway? Jessica is dead after all. I'm not being disloyal to her. Jessica would be happy knowing that Kenneth was being taken care of. Besides, that sort of thing happens in lots of cases: where the widower finds comfort, companionship, sex and love with old friends. Hey, what are friends for?'

But regardless of how many times she said these things to herself, she felt guilty and knew that Jessica would not be pleased with her actions; nor would Sybil and Sue. But that wasn't enough to make her stop.

The last time that she had seen Jessica's urn sitting around was when it was in his backpack, out at the burrowing owls site. She wondered where Kenneth now kept it, but it wasn't her place to ask and truthfully she would rather not see it, for it was just a reminder of how false-hearted she felt she had become.

There were few rooms in Jessica's house that Clarissa and Kenneth used together: the kitchen, Jessica's studio, and after the patio sex, he usually took her upstairs, past the master suite and the guest room that Kenneth occupied. He took her instead into the *other* guest suite, the same room in which Jessica's parents slept when they had often visited. The cobwebs grew thicker, wider and dustier over the dining room table, where five place settings were still laid out for dinner. It was obvious that Kenneth frequently used the one wing-backed chair in the living room, in front of the fireplace, but Clarissa was never invited to sit in the other chair that sat at an angle next to it. He didn't invite her into the family room either, where hung the rug-hooking and the painting that Jessica had made of herself and Kenneth, in the way she imagined herself and Kenneth might be in their senior years.

But because she was in love she saw none of this.

He would welcome her into the house with a smile, dance her along the foyer, feed her and had sex with her. He loved her, she thought. Though she never actually heard him utter the words. But he must love her for why else would he treat her so kindly? And why else would he want to be with her all the time?

Clarissa never had a problem justifying her absence from home, using the Blue Marble Club as an excuse. Cloe and Aiden hardly noticed that she was seldom there for like most kids in the modern world they were happiest to be left alone with an electronic gadget in their hands. They were content just so long as they were being fed. Jerry, on the other hand, from the moment that he got home from work flopped into his reclining chair. He had sat in it so often and for such prolonged periods of time that it even had a trained tilt that only long term use could give it. She and Jerry hadn't had sex for more than two months, not that she complained. Therefore even in the distant past when they did do it Jerry put little effort into the overall outcome anyway. Somewhere over the years their sex had lost that oomph that it once had. Yet, if asked, she could not recall when it became more effort than it was worth. Theirs was a predictable event and she knew the routine well. He'd ask, "Are you horny?" When Clarissa said 'no' he must have felt that it was too much bother to do a bit of foreplay and get her interested, for that was where it ended. Even when she said 'yes' he would crawl on top, pump away until he shot his wad, then roll over and sleep.

She had long ago decided, that without the satisfaction, why bother?

None of that mattered until she had had her first sexual rendezvous with Kenneth because before that, in her mind, they had a good, strong marriage. And she tried to explain it away by saying that 'it isn't all about the sex', which she had said so many times that she had almost convinced herself that it was true. However, since Kenneth had been having sex, she started looking at Jerry with disdain. And it took great restraint not to shiver when he came near. Then she would slam the door as she was on her way out to visit Kenneth. She wondered when Jerry had gained that extra fifty pounds. And why did all men have to fall into such a rut that all they thought about was whether there was adequate beer in the fridge and when the next game was on TV. Luckily for her, Kenneth wasn't like that. Jessica had said the same enough times as well. Now after all these years she could see it for herself. Kenneth was a good catch. Might even be a keeper.

Now when Jerry asked her if she was horny she said, "No." But she lied. For ever since Kenneth made love to her on that hot summer afternoon, she was horny all the time. Kenneth had tickled spots that she never knew that she had. In fact she once laughingly accused him of tickling her tonsils when he made love to her, for it felt like his penis had reached all the way up to her throat. Kenneth gave her the best sex that she had ever experienced and she wasn't about to do anything to sacrifice it.

And that meant that she could not tell Sybil or Sue where she spent most of her evenings and weekends. Little did she know that they were talking about her and Kenneth in the same way that they used to talk about Jessica and Kenneth, not that long ago: wondering, speculating and questioning what they were doing.

One evening Kenneth surprised Clarissa by asking, "How'd you like to take a trip to Wood Buffalo National Park?"

"Really? Whatever for? That's way up north by the Territories border." she said, excited by the offer without even caring about the remoteness of the park.

"I know, to see the whooping crane. They nest there. I've been studying them and I want to see how they live. Remember I showed you the book and played audio clips for you of the sounds that they make? There are more than two hundred that go there every summer. Of course we've missed the nesting period but that's okay, we can still see them with their chicks."

"When? When would you like to go?" She was ready to go at the drop of a hat and stay for a week if he had asked her. All she had to do was make one phone call to Rebecca, her store manager, to cover for her and then to do her packing. There, in her mind, it was already arranged.

"Next weekend. I've found a guide, outfitter and pilot who will take us in by float plane from Fort Smith, land on Lake Claire and they'll set up a camp in the marshland."

"You are so amazing Kenneth. I'd love to. Who else is going?"

"No one, just us."

Clarissa, exceedingly happy to spend a whole weekend with Kenneth, squirmed in her chair as she thought about making love to him under the stars, in complete isolation. She might even dance for him, naked for the open universe to see.

"Did you know that they are one of the few birds that will change their sexual partners?"

"No I didn't," she said, giving him a sideways look. Was there a hidden meaning in that statement?

"The males often change their breeding grounds in search of new partners to be as promiscuous as possible, to maximize his number of offspring and to widen the genetic pool," he mumbled on.

"I had no idea," Clarissa said, bored and uncertain if she even wanted to know where he was going with this. 'Or was he?' she wondered, immediately glancing at his cell-phone and remembering how many times she had wanted to get her hands on it, to see what he was up to before Jessica died. She shook off the idea and snuggled up to him. He wrapped his arms around her and all thoughts of snooping on his phone instantly vanished from her mind.

****

Clarissa had never imagined that the north, primarily the frozen north, could be so breathtakingly beautiful. Wood bison ran in herds across the vast open areas of sweeping grasslands that were criss-crossed with rivers and meandering streams. The undisturbed area of mosaic muskeg, sedge meadows and boreal forests, dotted with endless shallow lakes and bogs was so magnificent. It, like Kenneth, was mesmerizing.

"Look, Jessica. Look at the sea blight and the red samphire," he said, pointing out the window of the small plane. "They're of the few saline tolerant plants that will survive the salt plains. It should be easy to spot the whooping cranes against that red."

'Jessica?.... Did he just say Jessica?' Clarissa wondered. 'Was that a slip of the tongue after their thirteen years of marriage?'

When Clarissa remained quiet he continued, "We'll stop there on the way back. I can't wait to feel those salt crystals under our feet. Isn't this exciting?"

"Yes…. of course."

"Look, there's one. There's a whooping crane," Kenneth said, pressing his face against the window of the float plane. "Oh my, doesn't it almost take your breath away?"

"Yes, I'm breathless," she said, but she wasn't referring to the sight of the crane as she wondered why she had accepted this invitation. She had a sour taste in her mouth from Kenneth's mention of Jessica.

Clarissa was relieved when Blake, their guide, pointed and said, "Largest sink hole in the world."

"Beautiful," Kenneth said.

"Aboriginals roamed this land for thousands of years and still do," Blake said. "Gotta be a tough breed to live here."

As the plane landed Blake pressed a park permit into each of their hands. "You'll need to show this if asked by the authorities, though you're not too likely to see them way out here" he said, chuckling. "Let's get this gear unloaded," he motioned to his fellow-guide, Fred.

They stood with a pile of luggage and camping gear at their feet and watched as the float plane pulled away from the shore. "We won't see that pilot for another three days. Hope you're up for it," Blake said, with another chuckle. He had seen some people more anxious than ever to see that plane return after only twenty four hours. Fred and Blake always made a bet in that regard before the plane even left Fort Smith and to date they were running a fifty-fifty score.

It soon became clear that the site was used regularly because a tent for cooking was set up and two smaller tents for sleeping. "You and the Mrs. can use that tent," Blake said, pointing to the smaller of the two. "Fred and I will take the other."

"Any chance of seeing the whooping cranes tonight?" Kenneth asked, enthusiastically.

"Just down that way," Blake said, pointing southward. "Government won't let us near the nesting sites but a few hang around over there. I'll take you over while Fred sets up camp."

Kenneth tossed his and Clarissa's luggage into the tent, eager to see the first crane. "I read that they can live up to thirty years. Is that true?" he asked Blake.

"Sounds like you've done your homework," he said.

"Is there any chance of us seeing the northern lights?" Kenneth asked, eagerly wanting to know everything about this vast untouched land.

"Not at this time of year. Too many daylight hours," Blake explained, leading the way and walking along a narrow path that required the three of them to form a line. "You might see a Peregrine Falcon though, if you're lucky. Endangered too, just like the bison and cranes."

Kenneth only said, "Another one, I didn't know," filing this information in the back of his mind.

Clarissa shivered when Kenneth said 'another one' for that was the exact term that Jessica had used when Karen asked her to help save the Northern Leopard Frog. She momentarily wondered if it was it possible that this northern latitude was playing games with her mind.

They hadn't walked more than five hundred meters when Blake held up his hand, indicating that they were approaching the area where the whooping cranes fed. And there they were. The three of them stood transfixed for twenty minutes, hypnotized by the beauty of the four pairs of cranes. Mosquitoes and black flies swarmed around their heads.

Kenneth and Clarissa never did make love under the stars, as she had hoped. Nor did she dance naked under the moon. Instead she sat and watched the sun sink over the horizon while Kenneth noted down every move that the whopping cranes made. It was not quite the romantic run-away that she had imagined it to be. The bugs were so thick and annoying that no amount of bug spray could keep them away. On one occasion she mentioned to Kenneth that the mosquitoes were the size of fighter planes but he didn't even seem to notice them.

In fact she felt as though she was somehow being squeezed into Jessica's shoes and in all honesty they didn't fit very well. In her mind she could not get home soon enough. At least she had the mosquito bites to prove that she was in the wilderness for the whole of the weekend. And the wild romantic affair that she imagined did not happen so she didn't have to worry about telling that lie either. The whole arrangement put her into a slump.

CHAPTER THIRTEEN

KENNETH WALKED into Jeffrey's office the following Monday morning and said, gleefully, "You're not going to believe where I've been this weekend."

"I couldn't even imagine," he said, pleased to see that Kenneth was getting back to his old self.

"Wood Buffalo National Park."

"I thought there were only buffalo and mosquitoes up there," Jeffrey said, laughing.

"And whooping cranes and peregrine falcons."

"Did you say whooping cranes or whoopee?" he teased.

"Seriously, they're on the verge of extinction."

"So is your sex life. I'm serious. If I can sway your interests from the endangered species, we've got a special whoopee night planned and no whooping cranes in sight."

"When?" Kenneth asked, interested.

"Next weekend."

Kenneth thought for a moment. "I'll think about it," he said, smiling.

It had been five days since Kenneth and Clarissa had had sex. Unlike Clarissa he never gave their sex life much thought, for if it happened with Clarissa that was fine, and if it didn't that was fine too, until Jeffrey mentioned what his plans were for the weekend. He was actually more than ready for a whoopee night and at that thought he sent Clarissa a text message asking her to come by that evening. She replied within minutes, '*See you at seven* ☺'.

She was more than ready for sex, having felt cheated during their weekend at Wood Buffalo Park. Maybe it wouldn't have worked out too well making love under the wide open skies with all the mosquitoes and black-flies, but surely they could have had a good go at it in the tent if they had used enough bug spray. But the offer wasn't even there because he was too preoccupied with those fucking birds and mentioning Jessica's name one too many times.

When she thought about their affair she was disappointed that it didn't seem to be going anywhere but was more than happy to take what she could get. She would have moved in with him at the drop of a hat, given the option. But there wasn't even a hint of that. It just seemed foolish that they lived separate lives when sex was so good between them. On more than one occasion she had even considered going to a sex shop and picking up a long sleek vibrator to have on hand for the evenings when Kenneth didn't invite her to come by, but she never got up enough nerve to enter the shop. Unknowingly, Kenneth had increased her need for sex in the same way that he had done for Jessica.

In these past months Clarissa's friendship with Sue and Sybil seemed to have just slipped away. At first, when they called her and asked her to come by, she used the Blue Marble Club as an excuse, which wasn't totally a lie for she and Kenneth often talked about saving endangered species, in between making love. Now that they were having sex so regularly there was no time for girls' nights. It left no doubt as to where she would rather be. She certainly couldn't tell them what she was up to and was afraid that it would take but one look at her face and they'd know that she was having an affair with *someone*. Good sex added a special glow to her face and a sparkle to her eyes. One glance in the mirror assured her that she had it!

As usual, when Sue phoned her to invite her over, in the same week that she had returned from Wood Buffalo Park, she didn't want to go.

"Clarissa, I'd like you to stop over on Friday night," Sue said.

"Oh I don't know. I've was away last weekend and Jerry is getting pissed off that I'm always busy."

"Come on. We haven't got together for ages. It's long past time."

Clarissa knew that what she said was true. "Alright," she said, guiltily.

****

"What the hell is wrong with your face? You got chicken pocks?" Sybil said, failing a greeting and horrified at the partially healed bug bites.

"Oh that. They're getting better already. I was up at Wood Buffalo last weekend looking at whooping cranes if you can imagine. Those mosquitoes and black flies are a big as B52s. I'm completely exhausted."

"Here, this will get you back in shape. Sit. By the way, what have you been doing these past months?" Sybil asked, handing her a glass of wine.

"Mostly Blue Marble Club stuff," Clarissa said, knowing damned well that fucking Kenneth was hardly on the list of things that the club did. And aside from the leopard frog night and their little trip to see the whooping cranes she had done nothing that was directly related to the club. Of course there was that evening when she had had sex with Kenneth on the patio when they were supposed to be filling out the membership form, when she had screwed him for the first time. Of course, considering all those things, she could still credit some of it as club activities. In full truth she was only kidding herself, knowing that she had lied.

"Have you joined a fitness club? It sure looks as though you've lost a lot of weight," Sue asked.

"Gosh no. Are you kidding, I'm not organized enough to do that. Yea, maybe I've lost a few pounds. I've been really busy lately."

"Busy, with what?" Sybil asked, anxious to get to the bottom of it.

Clarissa blushed and said, "Oh, you know, the usual. The shop and such."

"Who are you trying to kid? Does Jerry know?" Sybil asked.

"Know what?"

There was a pause….. "What's his name?"

"Whose name?"

"Come on, we've known each other half a lifetime. Who are you seeing?"

Sue listened to their talk, her head turning back and forth, as Sybil quizzed Clarissa with yet another question and Clarissa flailed about, trying to answer.

"No one. Don't be ridiculous. You know that Jerry and I have a great relationship."

"So when was the last time he made love to you?"

"I don't remember. But we're not big on that. We have other stuff that keeps our marriage strong."

"Like what? Jerry watching TV and Clarissa watching Jerry watch TV?" Sybil baited her.

"Is that why I was asked to come over, for twenty questions?"

"Of course not," Sue stepped in. "But any fool can see that there is a glow on your face that wasn't there three months ago, even with all those bites. Sybil didn't mean anything by it. Maybe you're pregnant?"

"That's impossible. Jerry was fixed after Aiden. But honestly I wouldn't mind another," she said truthfully, as thoughts of a little Kenneth growing in her belly stirred in her mind. "You know that Aiden is eight already. I've sort of been thinking about whether or not we can have the knot untied. Either way, I wouldn't be the first one to get pregnant after the procedure. Those sperms have a way of slipping through. I'd actually be really happy."

"Knot untied? I hardly think that that is the procedure," Sue said, laughing.

"Well I don't really know but I've heard about people having it reversed. Maybe it's my age stirring up these thoughts," Clarissa said.

"Can't stop that biological clock from ticking, now can we?" Sue said. "But I thought that people only got the empty nest syndrome when their kids left home."

"I'm actually getting turned on just thinking about being pregnant," Clarissa admitted. "I liked being pregnant. I liked having a little life growing inside me."

"It's called lack of sex. When did you say the last time was?" Sybil teased.

"Oh Sybil, you're crazy. You're probably thinking about sex all the time because you and Nicolas are screwing like minks. Is he any good?" Clarissa asked, diverting the conversation away from her own self.

"I'd say pretty good. He's a keeper for sure."

"So what are your plans for a baby?"

"I think we're still practising. He hasn't popped the question yet and I'm not having a baby without a wedding ring."

"I don't blame you. I wouldn't either," Clarissa said.

Clarissa didn't really enjoy the visit with the girls. It wasn't like it used to be, not through any fault of theirs. She knew that it was because she was seeing Kenneth. She was too ashamed to admit it to them and liked Kenneth's sex too much to stop. Yet she didn't want to lose their friendship either. She knew that she couldn't have it both ways but she would play it that way for as long as she could. When she and Kenneth got married it wouldn't matter anyway for they would just make new friends. She thought.

Nor did she know that she had become pregnant. And only she would later know that it wasn't on account of Jerry's sperm slipping past the knot, as she put it. It was Kenneth's. In her case it was not that a baby was to be born out of wedlock, but that the father of the child was not her husband. Even worse....the father was the widower of her very best friend.

CHAPTER FOURTEEN

NO ONE could have been more surprised than Clarissa when Kenneth popped the question. And it wasn't the marriage proposal that she had hoped for. "How about we spice it up a bit?" he said. "We have an invitation to go out to dinner."

Clarissa was nervous about letting other people know that they were having an affair without a firm commitment from him, and asked cautiously, "Are you sure?"

"Absolutely. What do you say?"

"Alright, if you want it."

"So it's a date, Friday at seven."

When Kenneth said *Friday* warning bells went off in her head, her palms became sweaty and she felt faint.

"Are you sure you want to go out on a Friday?"

"Why not? It's as good a night as any," he said, excitedly. Little did she know that Friday night's dinner wasn't just a dinner date with friends, it would be Clarissa's introduction into *The Lifestyle*.

The next morning Clarissa was sick. She spent most of the morning with her head hanging over the toilet. She had always had a nervous stomach. She couldn't count how many times that she had eaten the wrong thing, on the wrong day, and it had spoiled her whole evening. Now it was this worry about having dinner with Kenneth's friends that had her upset. What if it was Jeffrey and Christine? They knew her. She puked again. She kept wondering why Kenneth had decided to flaunt their affair. Maybe wedding bells were ringing in the near future after all? Even though he hadn't asked her if she planned to divorce Jerry, it was naturally the next phase in their relationship.

As much as she had hoped for a proposal, she didn't want to do anything or say anything to risk losing him, so she didn't ask questions. She would happily attend the dinner party and be proud to be with him, even though, in between her vomiting she asked herself, 'Am I ready to let the world know what we are doing? Am I ready to sign the divorce documents after my fifteen years of marriage to Jerry?'

'Oh, how can I be ready for that if I'm puking my guts out?' she wondered. She was sick for the whole week. On Friday morning she sent Kenneth a text message to say that she was too sick to go to out to dinner.

Kenneth was not happy about this unexpected change in plans but in the end it didn't really matter if she joined him or not. He went to dinner alone.

****

Jeffrey greeted him at the door, surprised to see that he was alone, and said, "I thought….?"

"Yeah, I know. Something came up," Kenneth said, excusing Clarissa's absence without actually saying who was supposed to accompany him and why she had failed to attend.

Christine was as disappointed as Jeffrey to see Kenneth alone and gave her husband a questioningly-raised eyebrow. He brushed off her quizzical look with a sideways glance as they moved into the living room.

"I'll get drinks," she said, rushing to the dining room to remove one place setting before filling the wine glasses, not wanting to cause embarrassment

The evening went as Jeffrey and Christine had planned it, aside from the fact that it was a five-some rather than a six-some. Kenneth seemed to be back into the swing of things. After that night Jeffrey felt very confident that Kenneth would attend the next Callisto Akantha retreat in Montana. It was looking more and more likely that he would not be losing his deposit.

****

The following week Clarissa drove outside the city. She drove to the next town in search of a walk-in medical clinic. In her heart she knew the outcome but she couldn't bear hearing the news from her own doctor, whom she had been seeing for years and felt that the drive would do her good. For some quirky reason she also felt that it would also be easier to hear it from a stranger. She sat in her car for a full twenty minutes after she turned the car engine off, before she stepped out into the afternoon sun. On any other day, week, month or year she would have looked up and smiled at the warmth on her face. But today she was sullen and didn't see the wide expanse of blue sky overhead, hear the birds chirping in the trees or the babble of the brook as it raced along. For the first time in months she actually thought about Jerry, their years of marriage and what her future would hold. Tears streaked down when she turned her face up towards the sky and said, "I'm so sorry Jessica."

Within twenty minutes of walking into the clinic Clarissa was advised that she was six weeks pregnant. There was no doubt in her mind that the baby was Kenneth's. Now what does one do? She still had time to decide. She suddenly remembered what Kenneth had said about the whooping cranes and being at that *oh so wonderful* Wood Buffalo National Park, 'the males will often change their breeding grounds in search of new partners, being as promiscuous as possible, to maximize the number of his offspring.'

She groaned for she had wondered then if there was a hidden meaning in that statement. Had he been making reference to their relationship or was it simply a statement about the whooping crane? She now suspected that he had sex with her just to procreate.

'He is a manipulating, deceitful, self-indulgent, hateful bastard,' she said to herself as she stumbled back to her car. Yet as mad as she was at him, if he offered himself for sex right now she could not say no. She squirmed as she thought of how he touched her. It amazed her how he could give her a climax like no one had ever done or ever could do.

She hung her head over the steering wheel of her car and wept, loving him and hating him at the same time. In the end, having nowhere else to turn, she phoned her mother in Toronto.

"Mom, I know that this is short notice but I want to come for a visit."

"When?"

"Today. Now. Is that okay?"

"Of course, but are you okay?"

"I don't know. I'll be there as soon as I can get a ticket."

Jerry simply nodded when she said that she was going to visit her mother. Cloe and Aiden didn't say a word about it either and she wondered whether she would be missed if she never came back. Rebecca minded her clothing store on most days and welcomed the extra hours while Clarissa was away. There were orders that she should be placing but there was no way that she could stay. It was a long, sad flight home and Clarissa was never happier to see her mom's smiling face. She rushed into her arms and wept.

"Come on, let's get you home," Clara said, knowing that whatever was troubling Clarissa had to be serious. She never came home crying about anything, not even when she was in school, regardless of who had tried to bully her. She simply found a way to fight back. But today she seemed to have lost all fight.

Clarissa sat in her usual spot at Clara's kitchen table and ran her hand over it, remembering all those years as a child. She felt the little dips and grooves that had been created from the five generations that had used it. Cloe and Aiden had even left their mark on the day that they were fighting over a toy and a tiny dimple was on the edge where she now sat. She caressed it.

"Here you go love," Clara said, pressing a cup of tea into Clarissa's hand before sitting next to her.

Her mother had never sat on that side of the table and it felt awkward in a way, as if they were in someone else's kitchen.

"Oh mom, I've really done it now."

"How bad can it be, my dear?" she said. Clarissa's face was bowed and her mother tried to stroke her hair away from her face so that she could see her eyes.

"I'm pregnant with Kenneth's baby."

There she had said it, exactly as it was. No more pretending.

"Not Jessica's Kenneth? Your Jessica? Are you sure?" she said, astonished.

"Yes mom. I just don't know how it happened," she said, crying.

"Well perhaps it was when you and he got it on?" she said without thought, ever the outspoken parent. "I'm sorry to be so forward but that is the fact of it. Maybe you should tell me from the beginning."

"Well you know how Jessica always said that he was so perfect and we girls, Sybil, Sue and I, always said that her love for him was blind. I think that I've been blinded in the same way. This whole mess started after Jessica died, of course," she said, as if that made the situation better. "He convinced me to go out to see the leopard frogs. We sat there together in the setting sun and when I looked into his eyes I was completely besotted. From there it was just a touch, then a kiss and then he was slipping it to me. It was so beautiful that I couldn't stop. He would phone me and I'd be right there like a bitch in heat and spreading my legs. He made love to me and touched me in a way that was new to me. He stirred up a desire that I never knew that I had," she said, sobbing. "He is such an unbelievably good lover. I even went up to Wood Buffalo National Park to look at wretched whooping cranes with him and suffered so badly with bug bites that I had to get medication to clear it up. I would have done anything to be with him. I had even imagined dancing naked under the stars for him when we were up north. I hate myself. I am so stupid."

"Are you talking about Blue Marble Club stuff? I thought you had to be a member."

"It was his way of getting me to sponsor him. He's now a member, thanks to me."

"And now? Would you be with him if he asked you?"

"Probably, I ache for him so much," she said, rubbing her tummy where the new life was just beginning. "Now I have his baby."

"Well you don't have it yet. How far along are you?"

"Six weeks, tops."

"Then we have six weeks to make a decision."

"I don't know if I can do that mom. I can't even kill a spider."

"What would Jessica want you to do?"

"Now you're doing it. Everyone keeps saying: Jessica this and Jessica that. Jessica is dead and what does she have to do with this."

"More than you know. She is, or was, your best friend, your BBF…. you always said so."

"I know, but everyone keeps using her name, bringing her name up to manipulate others. I even did it," she said. "It's just been so hard without her. You cannot know what it's like to live without her. It's as if I've lost an arm or a leg. It hurts so much," she sobbed.

"There, there love," her mother said, wrapping her arms around her and patting her back. As stupid a thing as it was for Clarissa to do, she knew that Jessica's death had caused Clarissa to be with Kenneth. Clearly Clarissa somehow thought that by being with Kenneth that she was hanging onto Jessica. Reckless as it was, the baby was reality and now what? However, now was not the time to make a decision regarding the outcome of this pregnancy. She let it rest. "Let's get you settled: a nice hot bath and I'll make us a dinner. It will look different after some rest," she said, almost adding 'and being away from Kenneth', but she didn't.

Clara herself had been faced with more than one challenge in her life. The hardest was when her husband, John, Clarissa's father, died. Clarissa was only five years old when he was in a car accident. A drunk driver had broad-sided him when he was on his way home from the corner store. He had gone out for a jug of milk that they probably could have done well enough without that evening. It would have changed the whole sequence of events and perhaps he would still have been here today.

That terrible car crash left Clara to raise Clarissa on her own and to work at the same time. She had had her share of male offers but she had seen other single women stream men in through their doors and just when the children would begin calling them daddy they were tossed out on their ear. There was no way that Clara would have subjected her daughter to such things and in the end she remained a widow with a little antique shop to support the household. Of course finances were a bit tight from time to time but they had had a good life, just the two of them.

Clara and Clarissa had what most people called the perfect mother-daughter relationship, for they were also friends. But there was also a firm hand shown when necessary. From the time when Clarissa was young she spent more time in her mother's shop than at home or even with her friends. She liked hanging around with her mother and sitting in that shop that was filled with lovely old things passed down from generation to generation. She would polish and caress the furniture lovingly as if by doing so she could bring its history to life and hear the tales that might be told by its owners of long ago.

CHAPTER FIFTEEN

KENNETH HAD sent Clarissa his usual text message inviting her to come by. She replied to say that she was in Toronto and he never sent another, not even to ask when she was returning. She had no way of knowing that he was not sitting on his hands in her absence, not that she cared now. Without a second thought he had accepted another invitation from Jeffrey and Christine. He was more than pleased to know that Peter and Gloria, and Brian and Karen, would also be there.

****

That very next day Clarissa went to work with Clara, just as she had in childhood and through to young adulthood. She touched the collectibles that filled the shelves, before taking out the bees' wax to begin polishing the furniture, in the old familiar way. It felt as if she had never moved away for with each gentle rub the years seemingly vanished and she could think more clearly.

She certainly knew that it had been wise to come here. It was essential that she get away from Kenneth. Now with almost two thousand miles between them she could surprisingly see things so much more clearly. She was astonished to realize that he had manipulated her thoughts, desires and emotions. As she rubbed the wood to a gleaming shine she saw in it a reflection of herself and how her life was on the brink of destruction. She knew completely how Jessica must have felt that night when she wandered into the forest and then again during those last hours.

She cried for Jessica like she hadn't ever before. In her grief she knew that she would not, could not, keep Kenneth's child. But the options were few and hard: she could stay in Toronto until the baby was born and give it up for adoption or she could abort the foetus. Then she could try her best to forget the terrible mistake that she had made. And what of Jerry and her marriage?

As Clarissa polished the fine old wood she pondered if and when her love for Jerry had actually died. Was Kenneth her excuse to end a loveless marriage? Or was it loveless? Perhaps sex had simply reared its ugly head, yet again? And Kenneth a means to fulfill her sexual desires? She slammed her clenched fist onto the table, angry at herself for her own frivolousness and selfishness. The questions went round and round in her head. Clara looked up from what she was doing but left Clarissa to deal with her own torments.

Clarissa realized now, all too late, that it *was* all about the sex. Even now she ground herself against the chair attempting to ward off her desire as she recalled Kenneth's long hard cock slipping in and out of her pussy. Oh….. but she wanted him so badly right now. If he was just across the city she would have driven over to get the fix that she needed. In her heart she knew that he didn't love her, not that it mattered now. She felt foolish for imagining them as husband and wife. She had even been willing to sacrifice her friendship with Sue and Sybil. That made her the very worst sort of traitor in the world.

Oh sure, in the beginning she wanted it to be love……. but it was Jessica's love that she wanted. He *was* a wolf in sheep's clothing and she knew it. If only she could undo what she had done. If only she would have said no to his wanting to join the Blue Marble Club, and no to her taking him out to see the burrowing owls. It would have ended there.

Customers drifted into the shop from time to time and in between serving them with their purchases Clara sat across the room lovingly looking at Clarissa as the unpacked shipments of stock. She would periodically look up wishing that she could erase Clarissa's pain. But she also knew that Clarissa had to fight her own demons. When the tears fell from Clarissa's eyes Clara had to wipe her own away for she knew better than anyone that life was not always fair. When the crate was empty she walked over and stood behind Clarissa and caressed her shoulders.

When Clarissa cried, she held her. There was little else that she could do.

It was nice and easy to slide back into the old ways and their old lifestyle. They reassumed their mother-daughter relationship, where one didn't have to talk non-stop. Clarissa knew that her mother was there for her. Nothing had to be said. At the close of day they locked up the shop but didn't go straight home. Instead they did what they had done so many years ago, they strolled through the park. There were dozens of families out for the day, children running and jumping, playing on the swings and one or two crying from an unfortunate fall. They walked side by side and, were it not for the few wrinkles that Clara now had, they could have passed for twins. But the sadness that wrenched at both their hearts could not be seen. When Clarissa saw a tiny baby she placed a hand on her own tummy although she knew that it was much too soon to feel any movement.

Clarissa surprised herself when she said, "Let's go home. I would like to phone Cloe and Aiden." She had been away for days and this would be her first phone call to home.

Aiden picked up on the first ring and asked, worriedly, "Mommy, are you okay?"

"Yes I am, are you?"

"Daddy got me a new bike. It's purple and white."

Clarissa knew Jerry well enough to know that he had bought Aiden the bike simply to pacify him because she was away. Obviously Aiden was not dealing with her absence as well as he said he was. "And what did your sister get?"

"A new game for her computer and a new dress. Mine's better."

"I'm sure it is. It's nice to hear your voice."

"Derek and I are going biking. Here's Cloe," he said.

That made her smile.

"Mom, when are you coming home?" Cloe asked.

"Soon sweetheart. I just have to help Grams with a huge project first. But I'll phone as often as I can."

"I miss you."

"I miss you too baby."

"Daddy's here. Do you want to talk to him?"

"Maybe next time Grams is waiting for me. We have to go out," she told the lie so easily. She could not remember the last time that she had told a lie. Now she had turned into a regular liar. Another great attribute that she had gained from Kenneth. She ended the call and saw that Clara was just putting the tea onto the table. She simply shrugged when she realized that Clara had heard the lie.

"When are you going to tell him?"

"What?" Clarissa said, defensively.

"Jerry has a right to know."

"Know what? That I've been having an affair my best friend's widower? And that I'm pregnant with his child?"

"No…. That you don't love him."

"I never said that I didn't love him."

"Then why are you avoiding him? Why are you punishing him?"

"I don't know….. I can't think about Jerry right now," she said, stroking her tummy.

"I'm sorry. I shouldn't push you. But imagine being in his shoes right now. He's done nothing wrong."

"It's okay. I know that you're just trying to help."

CHAPTER SIXTEEN

CLARISSA DIDN'T receive any more text messages from Kenneth. She presumed that he had moved on to fresh pickings and was up to his old tricks again. In fact his disregard for her made it easier for her to deal with the awkward predicament that she was in. At that point, the last thing she needed was his advice. Not that he would have offered it anyway. She decided that his style would be simply to offer her a cheque to keep her mouth shut and leave her to take care of the nasty business on her own. Or worse for her to pretend that it was Jerry's baby and raise it as one of theirs. 'Heaven forbid that he should appear less than perfect in the circle of friends that he revolved in,' she thought, resentfully, knowing that in the end it was all about him. Well he had the perfect wife and he fucked that up royally now didn't he? because it was all about him.' Clarissa would always regret not checking out his favorite internet sites on his phone, before Jessica had died. She knew that she would never have another chance; not that it mattered anymore.

After his wild weekend with the usual group he was *back on track*, as Jeffrey put it. Although Kenneth could hardly recall what they had actually done, it was the soreness of his cock and the bruises that were a reminder that it was all good. He knew that the drug he had taken was not LSD but he didn't really care. He was simply looking forward to the next opportunity to indulge in his share of everything. He was more than ready for another Callisto Akantha getaway and he didn't need Clarissa around for that. After she had left town he thought of her as extra baggage and for that matter she certainly wouldn't be getting another text message from him or another invitation to anything. He could easily enough get a piece of ass at almost every turn. In fact there was a new girl in the office who had sparked his interest and he was formulating in his mind an offer that she could not refuse. Maybe he would have her work late one afternoon and give her a go on her desk?

His membership card, for the Blue Marble Club, arrived in the mail along with the dates and locations of the monthly meetings. Without thought of Clarissa he attended his first meeting and was surprised at the number of women who were interested in all that stuff. In fact there were only two other men in the group aside from Kenneth. One of them was clearly gay and Kenneth didn't hesitate in sidling up to him.
"Hi, I'm Kenneth," he said, almost calling him Pascal because he reminded him so much of that

beautiful man that he and Jessica had shared that night so long ago. "I just got my membership card last week."

"Vance," he said, offering his hand. "I've been a member for five years."

Kenneth shifted his backpack, the top slightly opened, showing the top of Jessica's urn. He took Vance's hand and gave him a good manly shake in return.

"Then you must know my wife, Jessica. It always feels so awkward whenever a person joins a new club. Almost like one's first day at school," Kenneth said, smiling. "Maybe we could have a drink after the meeting?"

Vance didn't add to what Kenneth said about Jessica and thought it odd when Kenneth had referred to her in the present tense. When Vance said, "I'd like that," Kenneth felt a tingle in his groin. Maybe there was a chance that he could get Vance interested in something other than a drink?

"I'm so pleased to meet you. It's people like you who make me glad that I joined the club."

Kenneth and Vance did go for a drink after the meeting and, like on so many other occasions of late, he left his back-pack in the car. The street lights cast a yellow glow over the parking lot and gleamed off the tall burgundy urn whose top stuck out of the pack. Although Kenneth had made more than one advance towards Vance it was obvious that they were only there for a drink. But that was okay, for Kenneth was a patient man and there would be other meetings and other opportunities. On more than one occasion he lost track of the conversation as visions of Vance and himself in a romantic setting overtook his thoughts.

The following morning he strode into Jeffrey's office and said, "That Blue Marble Club is quite the thing. You ought to join."

"Whatever for? I saw the bug bites that you brought home from up north and that shit isn't for me."

"I went to my first meeting and you should see the chicks. It's like a real smorgasbord," he said, avoiding any mention of Vance. "Some with knockers out to here," he said.

"I had no idea," Jeffrey said, uninterested. "Are we still on for Friday? Callisto Akantha, remember? We're going for the whole week. It's the annual big event and they hold special activities every day."

"Oh yea, Callisto Akantha: 'the nymph and the thorn'. How can I say no to that? I've got me a thorn that needs a nymph," he said, stroking his cock and thinking of Vance.

"I'd be happy to fix you up for now," Jeffrey offered, wanting to keep him primed for what was to come at the weekend.

****

Kenneth was much more excited about that weekend than he let on when he got in his car and he drove southward, leaving the city of Calgary behind. On the seat next to him was his back-pack and Jessica's ashes in her urn He tapped the pack and said, "They say that it's a lovers' paradise and that the best views are in early winter but I thought maybe a week in the summer would be a better time for us to get away. There's a nice lake, Lake McDonald. Also Heaven's Peak, I think it's called. You'll love it."

He popped a c.d. into the player and said, "Your favorites, Jessica. I made a copy from the stack on the c.d. player in the house. It would have been nice to bring the children along but they are at their grandmother's as they usually are in the summer. They do love it there," adding falsities that even he could not have explained.

Kenneth sang along with the songs: Remember, Memories and so many more that Jessica had loved. He thought about the great time that was planned for the weekend. Jeffrey and Christine had left the day before to make the drive, wanting to settle in and to do a bit of hiking before the events started. Kenneth would have done the same, but he wasn't much into hiking. But now that he thought about it he wished that he had researched the area a bit to see if there were any endangered species that he and Jessica would be interested in. Maybe they could make another drive down to check that out. It might also be the ideal opportunity to invite Vance along; after all he was a member of the Blue Marble. He smiled at the thought and when he reached over to place his hand over his pack, the top of the urn was hot to the touch and it scorched his skin as it had done once before. He suddenly realized his mistake in his thinking of Vance while she was next to him, and said guiltily, "All this wilderness is a great place to check out the wild animals. What do you think Jessica?'

He tapped his pack and said, "Of course just the two of us darling," while his thoughts drifted to Vance.

The retreat was at the south end of Lake McDonald and the crystal clear water underlined the untouched magic of the place. There wasn't a cottage or a home within a hundred miles of the buildings of Callisto Akantha's Retreat. Heaven's Peak stood at the north end of the lake and its snow-capped pinnacle was a reminder of how powerful the earth was to have created such a monument. He stood in awe looking at it until he remembered that he should move his things into his room.

Jeffrey and Christine were just returning from their hike when Kenneth turned to enter his chalet.

"I see you made it. Great," Jeffrey said.

"I'll just get settled and then I'll stop over, you're just next door I see," Kenneth said.

"Perfect, you should see the amazing hiking trails."

Kenneth dropped his bags onto the bed alongside his backpack and headed out the door. He didn't even bother to unpack for he was too interested in checking out the retreat. He stood admiring the view for a moment before bounding off the step and onto the front deck of Jeffrey's chalet.

"Welcome," Christine said, delightedly. "Come in and have a drink, then we'll do the tour. This place is enormous. There must be a dozen chalets and it's good that you reserved early. I heard that they're all booked up for the week."

"Wait until you see the program," Jeffrey said with a nudge. "Tonight is just drinks and getting to know one another, if you know what I mean?" he added with a wink. "Tomorrow is an all-girls night. The next is an all-guys night. Then there is the games evening. And that'll blow your mind…. I helped plan that," Jeffrey boasted. "Of course they have the toys event, too. And last, but not least, and this is new, you get to pick the partner of your choice. They're just trying it out to see if it's something that will happen every year. The perfect fucking specimen. Get it?" he said, nudging Kenneth's arm.

"Got anyone in mind Kenneth?" Christine snuggled up to him. "I think it's time we shone some light on my shame cave and you can do a little dippity-do-da," she said, grazing her fingernail over his breast.

"Of course, every event is optional and each has its own price tag," Jeffrey continued.

"Hey, if I was looking for a bargain I would have stayed home in Calgary and gone to Walmart," Kenneth said, laughing.

"And for afternoon activities we can go for a boat ride on the lake or take a hike up the mountain," Jeffrey said, as they stepped outside.

"You can bet that I won't be doing anything that may cause personal injury. I'm too afraid that I'll miss out on the events," Kenneth said. "I'll meet up with you later for the tour."

CHAPTER SEVENTEEN

THE ENTIRE compound was immaculate. Not just the chalets, but the entire set-up had a six star rating. Kenneth stood on the front deck overlooking the mountains like a great Earl surveying his estate. There were a dozen chalets in a circular layout with one enormous banquet hall in the centre backing onto the building that they called The Bordello. It was exactly as Kenneth had pictured it to be, except much more opulent than even he could have imagined. He smiled knowing that every chalet was full. This knowledge sent a tingling sensation down into his pelvis just thinking about what the week would bring.

"Ready for the tour?" Jeffrey asked as he and Christine stepped up beside him.

Kenneth nudged Jeffrey and whispered, "Do you mind if I get ready in your room this evening? I don't need any conflict on a week like this."

Jeffrey looked at him oddly and said, "Of course man. That's what friends are for."

"What was that all about?" Christine whispered when Kenneth went back inside for his jacket.

"Kenneth wants to get ready in our chalet. He mentioned something about not needing conflict while he's here."

"He's fucking brought her. Hasn't he?"

"What? Who?"

"Kenneth brought Jessica in that urn and he thinks that by getting ready over here that she won't know. He's still not right in the head. He's bonkers. I told you so. I can hear it now, *Oh Jessica love. I'm just stepping out for a bit of fresh air. I hope you don't mind*," Christine said, sarcastically trying to mimic Kenneth.

"Come on Christine. He's just grieving a bit… It's going to be a blast this week. Don't drag your own mood down on account of what Kenneth thinks and does. Besides he's usually the life of the party."

"Of course, you're absolutely right. I know that more than anyone."

****

There were twenty people at the retreat. Some, like Kenneth, came alone. From the moment that each walked through the door they were sussing each other out for the final night. Given the variety, there were more than adequate options for that experience. And even though that event was days away, when eyes locked and fingers brushed over skin it was the only thought in their minds. Fucking the specimen of choice. At Callista Akantha one didn't have to follow the old rule that said 'dance with the one who brought you'.

Kenneth was one of the more popular men and heads turned at his every move. His good looks, poise and confidence drew their attention like a magnet. He had an entourage of men and women alike that nuzzled closer to get near him. He liked that extra special attention and knew that he was not lacking in choices for the final evening. But let there be no mistake, he would be the one doing the choosing.

Dom Perignon champagne was served as introductions were made. Each guest was to stand at the call of their name, to introduce themselves and to tell the group what they liked or didn't like during sex. One could be as colorful as one chose to be, or not. At Kenneth's turn he said very honestly, "I am Kenneth and I like a body that is shaped with valleys and rises of soft smoothness. I also like a good hard cock and a silky sleek honey pot. And it doesn't matter in which order I get them," ending with a laugh making it very clear that he played sex both ways, and sometimes even both at once.

Cheers rose from the crowd as each guest stated their preferences adding their own personal cat-calls to color them up. By the time the evening was done Kenneth was positive that he knew who he was going to choose for the last night: Simone, the tiny blonde-haired beauty with blue eyes and a wide inviting smile. She was the image of Jessica.

By the time dinner was over Kenneth was more than ready for bed. All that thinking about sex was an exhausting situation. He went directly to his chalet, laid Jessica's urn on the pillow next to his and was asleep within minutes.

    The morning dawned with a bright blue, clear sky. There wasn't a ripple on the lake or a breath of wind. Even though Kenneth said that he hadn't planned on doing anything this week, aside from having sex, he couldn't resist the opportunity to get closer to that towering peak. Since hiking offered too much risk of physical injury it was not an option. As a compromise he decided to take the boat trip. He threw his back-pack over his shoulder, its top slightly opened and walked down to the dock. The boat was already loading and he stepped aboard. As luck would have it, the only available place to sit was next to Simone.
    "Kenneth," he said, introducing himself, "Sorry I didn't get your name. Is this seat taken?"
    "Simone," she said. "No it's not and yes, I'm alone." She spoke so softly that it was almost a purr.
    "Hey, there's nothing wrong with that," he said. "So am I," looking into her blue eyes, as he placed his back-pack at his feet and zipped the top shut before turning towards her. He was suddenly very pleased that he had chosen to take the boat trip.
    Kenneth was so captivated by this woman that for the first time in his life he was nervous and speechless. As the boat pulled away from the dock, a light wind blew through his hair and he sat next to her grinning like the cat that got the cream.

Simone would periodically turn towards him wondering why such a handsome man would be attending such an event, for certainly he could get any woman that he wanted. She liked his looks and his soft, gentle manner. She wondered if he was married when she saw that he was wearing a wedding ring, but this was not the place where one asked such questions.

Simone never would have registered for such an event, but for her best friend Sandra who pushed and pushed her until she enrolled. Even before she arrived at the resort she knew that she would be in way over her head if she participated in the events. But she hadn't come for that. The only reason that she had come was because the place had a five star rating and maybe, just maybe, she might meet someone.

Simone had never married. And marriage was not important. After seeing too many failed attempts she decided that it was not for her. On the other hand she would be more than happy to be a single mother. Things like that were neat and tidy; no strings attached. Her career as a Financial Advisor provided her with more than adequate means to support a child.

But in recent years she felt that her biological clock was ticking too fast and very soon would reach the point when she would never have a child of her own. She had even foolishly considered going down to the local pub to pick up some guy for a one-night stand, instead of spending the twenty grand at a sperm bank. Wisely she never did. And the only thing that steered her away was the thought that the one-night-stand-stud would recognize her at a later date.

Looking at Kenneth she decided that he just might be the specimen that she needed. Sandra was probably right in advising her to come here. All she had to do was hang around, sidle up to Kenneth a bit, maybe tease a little and spark his interest.

She stood leaning against the rail, turned, laid a hand on his arm and said, "Isn't that a beautiful sight?"

Kenneth jumped to his feet and tripped over his backpack just as the fog drifted back over the mountain top.

"It looks like you missed it," she said, sadly. "It'll clear again. I'm sure it will," she added, hopefully.

Kenneth kicked his backpack and flopped back down. "From now on you'll stay in the room," he whispered to himself.

"Sorry, were you talking to me?" Simone asked.

"No, I was talking to myself, I guess," he said, pushing the pack under the seat.

He turned and stood at the rail with her.

CHAPTER EIGHTEEN

KENNETH'S INTENTION was to participate in every event whole-heartedly. However, when he returned from the boat tour all he could think about was Simone. He imagined what he would do with her and the other women during the all-girls night and was most disappointed that she didn't show up for that. But within ten minutes of being there Christine, Cindy, Gloria and Karen, to name a few, brushed aside all thoughts that Kenneth might have for Simone. It was probably one of the most erotic times of his life watching them do each other, and him too of course, that he wondered if he would ever look at the act of sex in the same way again. He licked so much pussy that by morning he felt that he had perfected the art of cunnilingus. It was so beautiful that he just wanted to crawl right inside one of their vaginas. And on top of it all his beaver basher was so sore that he wasn't certain it would survive the week.

Kenneth had the option of having his morning breakfast served in his chalet, but unlike the previous morning, because he was still pissed off at Jessica, he left her urn on the corner of the dresser and went to the dining room instead. He was pleased to see that Simone was there and sitting alone.

He approached her table and asked, "Do you mind if I sit? I was hoping to see you last night," he said, without hesitation.

"I just couldn't," she said, ever so softly. She pretended that she was there for all the fun but never had any intention of attending the group sessions. What she had come for was an unwitting sperm-donor and she knew from the moment that she had met him that he was the one….. if she played her cards right.

"I know exactly what you mean. But I might have been able to turn it into a fun time for you."

"But then," Simone said, "I would have had to go to the other rooms as well and all those other men. You know the old saying, in for a penny, in for a pound?"

"I'm not much into tonight's event if you'd like me to stop over at your chalet," Kenneth lied, willing to forego a night of all men just to be with her.

"Is that kosher?"

"Why not? The last I heard it was one for all and all for one," he assured her.

Simone laughed and wriggled as the thought about his seed growing inside her. She couldn't have chosen better from any sperm-bank. She liked Kenneth's sense of humor and charming personality, as well as his good looks.

"I think maybe I could show you a thing or two," she said, trying to entice him.

"Well now. That's an offer that I can't refuse." Kenneth liked to do everything in an eccentric way. When he got down on his knees and said, "You name the time and I'll be there," she knew at that moment that she had lured him like a fish to a hook.

Simone's laughter was so sensual and soothing, like that of a stream flowing over a waterfall that he just wanted to slip inside her right now, and thoughts of the other entertainment were all but forgotten.

"So why wait? We can give it a go right now unless you have something else to do?"

"I'd love to but I have to wash my hair," she said, provocatively.

"I'm sure it will be well worth the wait," he said as she got up from the table.

"Until tonight. Is eight o'clock okay for you? Chalet number five."

The moment that Simone left the table Kenneth regretted that she would not make herself available right now. It would have been great to slip inside her that afternoon and join in on the guy's night as well. 'Hair-washing', if ever there was a put-off that was it. But just the thoughts of being with her were so appealing that he wasn't about to risk losing out. He would be patient. Eight o'clock would come soon enough.

He tried reading but couldn't concentrate, so with his back-pack slung over his shoulder he went for a walk and just before dinner he took a dip in the pool. Most everyone was hanging around the pool, either in the water or lounging in the chairs and sipping umbrella drinks, except Simone who he envisioned getting ready for him. The scene was exactly like that of being in the tropics until one looked up at the snow-capped peaks. He smiled at the thought of his and Simone's little secret. He lay back on the chair and imagined her soaking in the tub. He was certain that the scent of rosewater was in the air.

While he prepared for the evening, he put Jessica's favorite music on to play. He sang along with the words, dancing around the room telling Jessica how sorry he was that she had to stay in alone for he had a business meeting to attend.

The last thing that he did before stepping out for dinner was slip a little blue pill into his pocket to take as he left the dining room. When he entered the dining hall he was again surprised to see that Simone was not there. He immediately tensed up and wondered if she had changed her mind, then relaxed as he convinced himself that she was just preparing herself for him. That thought renewed his enthusiasm and he had to uncross his legs to make himself more comfortable. Although he had had more pussy last night than ever in his life he was hornier then than he could ever recall.

He had waited ten minutes outside her door, pacing back and forth, not wanting to be early and appear too anxious. The scent of lavender drifted out from the open window and Stravinsky's 'Rite of Spring' was playing. It sent his heart racing for he knew the music all too well. It was the music that Jessica used to play when she was having an affair with her personal trainer, Blaine. It made him so sexually aroused that he had to brush his stiffening cock down. He swallowed the little blue pill knowing that it would add hours to his performance. At exactly eight o'clock Kenneth knocked.

When Simone opened the door for him, wearing a burgundy and white corset with holes cut around her nipples, he knew that it must also have an opening in the crotch. He was on cloud nine.

Without thinking he said, "Oh Jessica, my Jessica." It felt to him as if he had slipped back in time, back to another occasion. It was as if he had the opportunity to experience his Jessica all over again.

Simone looked at him questioningly then laughed. She didn't care what he called her just so long as he planted his seed deep enough for it to catch. She placed a glass of wine in his hand and said, "Cheers, here's to us."

"Oh yes, my angel. To us." He swept into the room and danced with her to the music. He was breathless when he said, "Sit, Jessica, how sweet the moonlight sleeps upon this bank. Here will we sit and let the sounds of music creep in our ears."

"Shakespeare?" Simone said, surprised, wondering where that had come from.

"Yes, my Jessica. Soft stillness and the night become the touches of sweet harmony. Look how the floor of heaven is thick inlaid with patens of bright gold."

"Kenneth. I'm not Jessica. I'm Simone," she said, suddenly afraid of him.

"Yes my sweet, walk with me down the river of love, open your heart to me and let me touch your soul," he said, as he grazed a finger over her breast and kissed her lips.

She squirmed. At that point she could not have said no to Kenneth even if she had wanted to. She took his hand and placed it over her pussy. He weaved his fingers though its silken hair. It was soft and swollen, hot and moist. She was ready for him. Eagerly they removed his clothes, anxious to brush skin to skin.

Kenneth made love to Simone like no one had ever done in her life before. He touched her and caressed her ever so gently and erotically that she began to believe the words that he uttered. She clung to him, not knowing that it was exactly the way that Jessica used to.

And just before her climax he asked her, "Open your eyes so that I can see them go from blue to grey."

She opened her eyes and looked into his. They climaxed together. Kenneth felt as though he had shot his seed into the heavens. Simone clung to him. He rocked her back and forth and wept, "Jessica, my love, it's been too long. I love you so much."

The following morning Kenneth was beating on Jeffrey's door. "Hey sleepy-head, the sun has been up for hours and you're wasting the day."

"Kenneth, is that you. Come on in."

Christine was still asleep.

"Hey, where were you last night anyway?" Jeffrey said, wiping the sleep from his eyes.

"She came back to me. Last night Jessica and I made love."

"I don't know what you've been smoking but you know that's not possible."

"I'll bring her by and you can see for yourself. Today. This afternoon. It was so beautiful."

"Hey man. I don't know what you're talking about but I need some rest. I've never been fucked like I was last night and I'm not going to miss one minute of tonight. You have no idea what you've missed. It's games night. You'll be there won't you?"

"You know that I can't go. She won't like it. Remember last time? I'm not going down that road again."

"Whatever…. just go away," Jeffrey said, totally exhausted.

Christine was awake when Jeffrey crawled back into bed. "What the hell was that all about?" she asked.

"You're right. Kenneth is losing it, he was muttering about having sex with Jessica last night."

"See? It's what I told you. He might be a good fuck but I think he's misplaced a few marbles with Jessica's death. He is coming tonight isn't he?"

"Who knows? I can't imagine him missing the games-night. He paid for it but something tells me that he's not."

Neither Kenneth nor Simone attended any other activities for the rest of the week. They ate their meals together in her chalet. They spent the afternoons together going for nature walks and they fucked each other's brains out in the evenings and through the night. As far as Simone was concerned Kenneth was the perfect specimen, in more ways than one. And what did it matter that he called her Jessica, it was a nice name and every time he shouted her name he sank his cock ever deeper and it seemed to increase in size. Who could say no to such a performance? Certainly not Simone.

At the end of the week Simone felt downright pleased as she was leaving, closing the door to her chalet. With her suitcase in one hand she turned back to look at the various chalets that made up the retreat, the crystal blue lake and the towering peak. She smiled for she felt good about the way things had seemingly fallen so perfectly into place.

Kenneth was crossing the yard, saw that she was leaving and raced over to her. "Where are you going? You can't leave," he said. "You have to come home with me Jessica."

She simply said, "You know that that goes against the rules."

"Rules are made to be broken. I can't live without you. I love you Jessica. I must have you," he said, shouting loudly.

Jeffrey heard Kenneth's raised voice and rushed over. "Hey man, what's up," he asked, placing a firm grip on Kenneth's arm and turning him away from Simone.

"I can't bear to lose her again," Kenneth said, weeping.

"Here's Christine, let's go have a drink," he said. "Relax man. We've been having a good time, right? Let's not spoil it all now."

George and Cindy, Peter and Gloria, and Brian and Karen were on Christine's heels. Within seconds they had crowded around Kenneth allowing Simone to run down to her rental car and drive away without his noticing. She prayed, hoping that there was no way that he could trace her, as she sped her way through the mountains and to the airport, wondering if she had accidently told him her last name. The moment that she was within cell phone range she stopped the car, signed onto the Callisto Akantha website and deleted her membership.

It took more than an hour for Kenneth to calm down and the first thing that he did was go into his chalet and get Jessica's urn. He placed it inside his shirt and flopped into a chair. The silky smoothness of the metal was cold at first but very soon it warmed where it rubbed against his skin. He seemed oblivious to its sharp base as he rocked back and forth saying nonsensical things. His friends stood around him reliving the night that Jessica had died. Only this time it was much worse. He had a wild look to him that they had never seen before and they feared the worst.

There was little that they could do to ease Kenneth's pain, aside from being there for him. Peter drove Kenneth's car for him while he sat slumped in the passenger seat, weeping and hugging the urn to his body. The other four cars followed behind like a convoy. If there ever was a time when Kenneth needed friends it was today.

When they had met Simone days ago they each saw her similarity to Jessica. At the time they thought that it was unnerving but they never imagined that it would lead to this. Maybe they should have listened to Christine? for ever since Jessica had died she had been saying that Kenneth was deranged. Now it was more than obvious that she was right. Jeffrey considered taking Kenneth directly to the hospital. But in the end he simply drove him home.

CHAPTER NINETEEN

KENNETH REFUSED to allow anyone to stay in his house with him. He kept muttering something about, "Jessica wouldn't like having you lot around." Only he knew the enormity of the truth in that statement. If only he had listened to her. He missed her so much.

He wandered from room to room, carrying Jessica's urn with him. When he felt hunger he did not want food. When he was thirsty he could not drink. And when he was tired he could not sleep. Something had sapped his strength and, try as he might, he could not work it out. 'Maybe I've been working too hard?' he wondered, in his confused haze.

Within days of Kenneth's return from the Callisto Akantha retreat he decided that all of his problems *might* be associated with an addiction to sex. Maybe it was all about the sex? If not for the sex he would never have attended the Callisto Akantha retreat. He knew in the back of his mind that he certainly had *a* problem and that was the best analysis that he could come up with. He had heard about such afflictions and given that he was only human it was possible. And he could not deny that he did love sex. Ever since meeting Simone he had had almost a constant hard on.

He wondered when his weakness had begun. When had things starting feeling out of sorts? Yet try as he might, he could not pin it down. As he pondered that matter he stroked Jessica's urn. The silky smoothness of it caused his cock to harden even more as he thought about having sex with Jessica. He was hard and ready. Without hesitation he did what he had done every day in the privacy of their home, ever since Jessica had died. He stripped naked and ran a bath. He scrubbed every part of his body completely and thoroughly before drying his skin vigorously. While he did that Jessica's urn stood on the edge of the bathroom counter.

"See Jessica, all clean. All that bad stuff is washed away. I'm clean for you. Just for you sweetheart."

Kenneth then lathered himself with body oil. His skin was shiny and silky smooth.

"Of course I want you, see how hard I am," he said, stoking its length. "I'm going to slip inside your silky pussy and move back and forth just the way you like it. Slow and easy."

Clutching Jessica's urn he turned and walked into the bedroom. He lay on the bed and manipulated his nipples with the urn while stroking his cock with his other hand. He slipped the pocket pussy over his cock and bucked against it.

"Oh baby I love you so much. My Jessica," he said, rolling the urn up and down his body and touching it to the tip of his cock. It felt hot and sensual against his skin.

"I'm coming baby. Can you feel my fullness inside you? Oh Jessica, my love," he groaned, climaxing.

He lay like that waiting for his heart rate to settle, rolling the urn up and down his body. He left it in the bedroom when he went downstairs and into Jessica's studio. What he had to do next was not for her ears.

He opened the phone book to the yellow pages, searching for a sex therapist. There was a list of six Registered Clinical Psychologists. A wide red circle was drawn around the name Caroline Walker, BJ, MA, RPsych and someone had written the words 'sex addiction' in bold letters beside the circle. In a moment he knew that it was Jessica who had written those words. It sent a shiver down his spine. He read through the names of the other therapists but his eyes kept going back to Caroline Walker's phone number. He closed the book, frustrated, and turned on his computer. He did a search on sex addiction. There was very little to be learned aside from the fact that it was a real issue in the westernized world. It was also noted that people with a tendency towards any and all addictions were most likely also to become addicted to sex. It had long been known that people from all types of societies have had an overwhelming interest in sex from kings and queens to paupers. But the most talked about addictions occurred in wealthier families. And internet sites had opened up a whole new world for anyone wanting or needing sex. Kenneth himself was a prime user of that source.

He had never been addicted to anything before in his life, unlike his loser brother Matthew who had spent time in the pokey for trafficking drugs, following a lifetime of petty crime. Sure he had to admit that he had taken a few drugs in his time but that was just to spice up the night. It was only done amongst friends and did not amount to much. Kenneth was also more than happy to have the odd glass of wine or two but again it was only when he was with friends. Sure there was the odd occasion when he had perhaps slipped into a drunken haze. But he thought that that was hardly a sign of addiction.

He looked back at the phone book and wondered if Jessica had experienced the same physical need as his. Why else would she have circled the number and written those words? For just a moment he considered going back upstairs and talking with her about it but in the end it didn't matter. At least they were keeping it in the family.

He opened the phone book again and wondered what kind of anxiety Jessica had endured. He had loved having sex with her. And the way that she shouted the roof down made it obvious that he could pleasure her. But in his mind, though not a feeling shared by her, the best sex was when they went to the Callisto Akantha retreat and there were seven people making love to her at the same time. If anything might cause an addiction it would be that, *the ultimate sex*. Forgetting that it was Saturday and the office was closed he dialed Caroline Walker's office phone number. After four rings it went directly to voice mail. It indicated that in the case of an emergency one should visit the local hospital. Kenneth laughed and thought, "My case would hardly be classified as an emergency. They'd just tell me to take two aspirins and have a good fuck."

He hung up without leaving his number, not remembering that his identity would show on call display and that the office had a system whereby they could cross-reference phone numbers to client's names. They would know in an instant that Kenneth's call was linked to the file of Jessica Lund.

After making the call he thought of nothing else besides sex and he didn't even bother to get dressed. He wandered from room to room with Jessica's urn under his arm and rubbed it against his skin. He wore the pocket pussy fulltime and at the moment when he could stand it no longer he would lie where he was and in his mind have sex with Jessica. He could not get enough of her.

****

On the same weekend that Kenneth tried to make an appointment to see Caroline Walker, Sue phoned Sybil.

"I know that it's probably too late but we've got to do something. I've been shopping all week for what we need and I think I have it all. I need you to come over right now."

"Sue, what's going on?" Sybil asked, half afraid.

"I don't mean to scare you, but we have good reason to be nervous. We should have done the spell on him right away when he caught Clarissa's eye. Hell, we should have done this for Jessica too."

"Should have done what? What's going on? And what do you mean…. a spell?"

"You'll see. But we have to be totally alone. Leave Sukie at home too."

"Sukie…? What's my dog got to do with this? Are you okay…? I'm hanging up right now."

"I'll be ready for you in ten," Sue said, and ended the call.

Sue's call did puzzle Sybil but she did as she was told and for the best interest of Sukie she took her to a neighbors' place. Ever since Sybil had known Sue she had thought her to be one of the better grounded person that she had known, so whatever was going on today was a bit over the top. Sybil drove up and saw that Sue was wandering around her yard, sprinkling ashes around the perimeter of the house. She was wearing a long flowing black gown and had a long line of bangles on her wrist. Her hair was tied back with a wide band and her eyes were dark having outlined them with kohl.

"Holy smokes! Look at you. Should I have dressed up too? What is this? Halloween?" Sybil asked, nervously.

"No silly… and you look great as you are."

"What are you doing?"

"Protecting the perimeter," Sue said, leading the way into the house.

"Are you okay?" Sybil asked, still puzzled.

"I'm fine. It's Clarissa I'm worried about. I'll never forgive myself for not doing this for Jessica."

""Pardon my ignorance but what the hell *are* you doing?"

"We're turning the fires of hell onto Kenneth."

"Sue…." Sybil said, sighing heavily. "I know that you mean well, but how can Kenneth receive what he deserves from all this craziness?"

"It's not craziness. It's magic. Black magic," Sue added, confidently.

"You and black magic," Sybil said, looking at the table that was filled with needles, feathers, tabasco sauce, candles, a sharp knife, a pair of beads, a bottle of sherry, a bowl of strawberries, a dish of soft chocolate and a five foot long boat-tiller. "What the hell is that?" she asked, pointing to the tiller.

"A boat-tiller, we've got some steering to do."

Sybil laughed and said, tongue in cheek, "You are so funny. I love you. You've already got me believing that this will work."

"Then toss the wax into that pot and put it in the oven. Set it on low. We're not melting it, just softening it. We've got some manipulating of Kenneth to do."

"I never thought I'd see the day," Sybil said, her eyes twinkling in astonishment.

"We've got to bend his brain and get Clarissa out of his head. And for sheer punishment he is never going to look at women in the same way again."

"What's he done with Clarissa?"

"He's bewitched her that's what he's done. I've known it for a while. I'm just scared that we've waited too long like we did with Jessica."

"What are you talking about?"

"If I've measured it correctly you were right. Kenneth's got her pregnant."

"You are kidding me, right?"

"I wish I was. What have you got of Jessica's? I have her picture," Sue said, propping it up on a cushion at the kitchen table.

"I have a barrette," Sybil said, taking it from her hair. "And her high school ring. I stole it from her jewel box when I was in the house getting Brianna's and Simon's stuff."

"Would you mind getting me a pot of honey and please unplug the phone. Heaven help anyone who tries to disturb us tonight." Sue said as she placed Jessica's ring on the table in front of her picture, together with the barrette. She then drizzled honey over both objects.

"Okay, let's get on with it," Sue said. "The wax only needs to be pliable not melted, so would you mind checking it," she said, nodding towards the stove.

"I think it's almost there," Sybil said, opening the oven. "Just tell me what you need me to do." She could hardly supress a smile.

"I need a snippet of your hair," Sue said, making the cut, ended up cutting an extra-long piece of her hair and placing it on the table. "Perfect, long strands are the best. Mine too of course," she added, cutting a piece of her own.

"How can this possibly work?" Sybil asked, wryly.

"Believe me, this will work. I'm no babe-in-the-woods when it comes to this stuff."

"Really? I'm impressed."

"Damn I hate myself for not protecting Jessica, but we believed her. If I teach you nothing else, always trust your instincts. While I get things in order I'd like you to make a list of how we're going to fix Kenneth."

"I don't know what to write. I've never done this before."

"Just write down all those things that Kenneth needs punishing for."

"Well hey, now you're talking. I can list a dozen in two minutes flat."

"That-a-girl. I knew you had the right stuff," Sue said, smiling.

"Aren't you going to cover your table with something, this wax will do a number on it," she said as she watched Sue drawing the outline of a pentagon on the kitchen floor with chalk.

"Don't worry about that old thing. I'm not taking a chance on doing anything that will reduce the power."

At the points of the pentagon she placed five white candles and one black one in the center of the table, with feathers scattered over the table top.

"What are you going to do with that antique Genie bottle?"

"We're going to bottle and seal up Kenneth's remains along with his punishments."

"But I thought you wanted to have your ashes put into it when you die."

"That was then and this is now. This is much more important. There," she said, "The only other thing that I need is a rope. Kenneth doesn't know it but he's hung himself out to dry."

"Here, use this thing," Sybil said, handing her a braided rope from her hair. "It's a favorite of mine,"

"Perfect. Everything's ready. When I give the word you can drop in your list of punishments," Sue said, lighting the candles. "The sun will be setting in fifteen minutes. Now bring me the wax. We're going to shape us a Kenneth and then he's going to choke on his own venom," she laughed.

"Really? What are you going to do to him?"

"You'll see, all in good time….. it's long overdue that he gets his come-uppance."

"Like making him impotent?" said Sybil, daring the pun.

"That's a good start. I take it that it's on your list. It's on mine too. If you'd do the honors and pour us a shot," she said to Sybil.

"My pleasure," Sybil said, pouring them a generous shot of sherry.

"To Jessica and Clarissa," they toasted. Then Sue started to shape the wax into that of a man.

The feathers rose and fell from the table with the air movement. The bowl of strawberries and chocolate stood next to Sue's Genie bottle and the black candle. Sue shaped the head and on it she placed two black beads for his eyes. "Okay you stick the hair on the head while I form the body. Get it stuck in there really well. We've got to get into his brain."

"Is that okay, like that?"

"Perfect," Sue said, shaping the trunk and an attached penis. "When you've done that, get the Tabasco sauce ready and hold that needle over the flame."

"What's it for?"

"To make a hole in his dick. He's going to be pissing fire really soon."

"Really? What for?"

"Figure it out."

"No way! You're going to burn the end of his thing off?" she giggled.

"That would be just too bad now, wouldn't it?" Sue said, scathingly.

"I so hope that this is going to work. I love it already."

"Okay, bottoms up. If we're going to pull this off we need all the help that we can get," tossing back the drink. "Chocolate coated strawberry?" Sue offered one to Sybil.

"Oh, they're for us? I was hoping they were."

"Eat your heart out Kenneth Lund and hang onto your britches. This is the night that you've been waiting for," Sue said.

"You *are* actually pouring that stuff on the end of his thing. Oh… my…. gosh, this is great." She laughed.

"Okay, now drop your list in the bottom of the Genie bottle with mine and you need to tie that rope really tightly around it while I put him in there."

"Okay. But you're melting Kenneth again? Holy smokes look at that." Sybil said, astonished at how rapidly Kenneth was softening and dripping into the bottle."

When all the wax was melted into the Genie bottle Sue said, in a voice strange and unlike her own, "Get that cork ready and hold your end of the rope. Don't give him a chance to get out. Now, pull that rope tighter and hold that tiller straight. We have to make sure that he only goes where we steer him."

Sybil was trying hard to keep her face straight.

Finally Sue said, "Okay it's done."

"So what's going to happen to Kenneth?"

"Don't ask. You don't want to know. Besides you'll hear soon enough."

"And what about Clarissa?"

"She'll be home soon."

"What about Kenneth's baby?"

"It's as good as dead. But you didn't hear it from me. And our sweet darling Kenneth will never think about women in the same way after tonight. Well maybe not tonight, but he'll get his just desserts in the end."

****

Kenneth bolted out of his bed, holding his cock and balls. "Jessica, what are you doing?" he yelled, glaring at her urn. He was sound asleep when the end of his penis felt as though it was on fire. Clutching his balls he thought that they felt swollen. He stood before the mirror and moved his limp penis out of the way and sure enough, his balls were swollen to almost twice their normal size. He fell to the floor from a sudden stab of pain in his heart, another on his foot and another to the side of his head. He looked around the room certain that an intruder had gotten into his house, though he couldn't imagine how or when. Just as that moment he clutched his legs for it felt as though his feet had been severed at his ankles.

He cried out in pain, feeling as though someone was squeezing his heart. A dozen streets away Sybil and Sue tugged even harder on the rope as they tightened Sue's rope around his neck, cutting off his very breath. It was more than he could bear. Kenneth rolled back and forth on the floor clutching and grasping at the invisible rope. Finally he fell into a deep sleep.

He only regained awareness, his suffering ended, when the last of the candles sputtered and died, a few hundred yards away. Kenneth walked through every room of the house, stumbling and cursing, certain that a thief was just beyond the door to the next room. The only room that he didn't and wouldn't enter was the master suite. When there wasn't an intruder to be found he decided that what he had experienced was simply a most vivid nightmare.

Kenneth was terrified to sleep after that. Every light was left on and he would double check the security system countless times throughout the day and night. He would repeatedly put his hand to his throat for it still felt a painful pressure. Although he had felt as if he had been in a bar brawl, there wasn't a bruise or mark on his body. After two sleepless nights he placed a second phone call to Caroline Walker's office. He had no idea what all the letters meant behind her name, BJ, MA, RPsych, but the more diplomas the merrier for he wanted the best qualified person to take care of him. He again wondered if his constant desire for sex was bending his mind and had caused all that pain.

The burning sensation on the end of his penis that he had suffered since Saturday night had been reduced to being *almost* bearable. At one moment he considered calling his family doctor. He wondered if maybe he had got some kind of disease. Yet that was hardly possible since he hadn't had sex since Simone and that was more than two weeks ago. She was not just angelic but divinely pure he was sure.

Little did he know that his self-diagnosis was certainly on the right track for it was certainly sex related! But in his case it was due to having sex in all the wrong places and for all the wrong reasons.

Kenneth's call was answered on the second ring and knowing that he had an appointment to see Caroline Walker he instantly felt enormous relief. Ever since he had had that horrible *nightmare* all interest in sex had faded away. He smiled. Maybe the nightmare had cured his sex addiction, if he even had an addiction at all. He looked at his pathetic, shrunken dick, rubbed Jessica's urn over its tip and flicked his nipples. Nothing... zero. He had absolutely no desire or need for sex. He was almost tempted to call the office again and to cancel his appointment but in the end he decided against it. Maybe there was something to be learned from Ms. Walker. In fact he liked the idea that he would be seeing the same therapist that Jessica had chosen.

Caroline Walker had opened her own clinic ten years ago, right after she had received her degree. Her major was in drug addiction, though in her mind there was very little difference in treating addicts regardless of whether it was drugs, alcohol or even kleptomania. But her biggest challenge in the past couple of years was the growing number of clients seeking therapy for sex addiction. Of course it had been a part of her study, but at that time there was limited knowledge and no case studies to work from. That left it difficult for therapists to provide proper counselling. More recently there had been more advanced studies and almost daily she would receive updated information. Yet in her mind she couldn't see how such an addiction could really exist. Sex is sex, a normal human activity. Sure, some sex was better than others. She knew that well enough for she was no virgin when she got married. But to be addicted? The whole concept left her baffled and doubtful. It worried her that she herself had a growing number of clients. Yes, strangely enough it did seem to be a growing perceived problem.

Although she liked to believe that she had an open mind yet, with her very straight background, she was well outside her comfort zone when it came to the topic of sex. She had difficulty talking about it, especially about what people actually did during the act of copulation. She and her husband had always maintained an active sex life and it was more than adequately satisfying. But it was not very adventurous and they rarely strayed from the missionary position. She felt as though she was one of the lucky ones who enjoyed the experience of a climax and had a husband who ensured she was well satisfied.

So far, and luckily for her, most of her clients' concerns were dealt with in a civilized manner consisting of an almost refined discussion. As a result, Caroline was able to state, very proudly, that she had yet to see a client for a second consultation for sex addiction.

Caroline's secretary, Bertha, had pulled Jessica's file and made up a new file for Kenneth. Caroline knew that it was common for both partners to be affected by the same addiction: drugs or alcohol or whatever it might be. She read the last of the notes on Jessica's file and closed it. At that moment she had no way of knowing that Jessica had committed suicide months ago.

Kenneth strode into Caroline's office, ever confident and cocky. He was no longer that beaten down person who had made the appointment.

"I will be taking notes for your file," she courteously informed him, removing her wide rimmed, red colored reading glasses when she turned to look at him. She was surprised at his amazingly good looks and confident manner.

"I don't really see why that's necessary," he said. "This will probably be my one and only appointment. I think I've taken care of my problem," shifting his still limp penis and swollen balls uncomfortably.

"I see. Well, this is my procedure and, in the event that you should decide to return, it will be helpful," she said, ending further discussion on that matter and putting her glasses on again. Kenneth decided that that was a nervous habit of hers.

"Very well, go ahead," he said. "You're probably recording every word anyway."

She didn't respond to his rude comment but simply made a note on his file, in reference to his rudeness. "I would like you to be comfortable. You may sit in the chair that you're in," she said, not mentioning that it was the exact same chair that Jessica had used. "Or you may lie on the sofa."

"I think I'll take the sofa. It will make it feel more like the real thing," he said, getting up and making himself comfortable on the sofa. "Should I close my eyes?" he asked, "Like they do on TV."

"Only of it'll make you feel more comfortable," she said, smiling. He was a charmer.

Caroline moved to a chair and asked, "So let's begin with why you've come to see me."

"I've done some research and think that maybe, just maybe, I'm addicted to sex."

"Have you always been addicted to sex?" she asked.

He glanced at her and saw a look of amused skepticism.

"Well probably not always but I've always liked sex."

"Liked it in what way?"

"I really like to do it. I like to slip my cock inside Jessica's silky pocket."

"Jessica is your wife?"

"Yes."

"Have you had sex with other women?"

"Of course, I'd be a fool not to from time to time. And what man hasn't?"

"And do you have sex with men too?"

"Oh sure and that's pretty good as well," he said.

"When did you start having sex with men?"

"Shortly after Jessica had Alicia join our love triangle. It wasn't long after that when she asked Pascal to come in. Ahhhh yes he sure did come in," he said, wiggling against the sofa.

"And you didn't have anything to do with this?"

"Of course I did, but she doesn't know. I sort of coerced her you might say. We needed to spice it up. And she loved it."

"Did she love it or was it all about you."

"Both I guess, at first."

"Most couples will use toys to keep the sexual aspect of their relationship alive."

"We did that too, early on. I guess you could say that it escalated."

"I see. And what kind of sex do you prefer?" she asked noting the details on the file.

"Group sex, of course. It goes without saying. Or at least I used to. When Jessica went off it I changed my taste as well, so we don't do that anymore."

"I see," she said, so it had gone that far. She remembered Jessica implying as much. She continued with only a slight pause, "You should also know that the DSM, or the Diagnostic and Statistical Manual of Mental Disorders, used by all psychiatrists and psychologists, does not consider sex addiction to be an addiction at all. Yet it has been described as having very similar compulsive behavioral characteristics to those of a compulsive jogger, or a video gamer. You might even say that a strict vegetarian is suffering from an addiction."

"Well I'm no expert on jogging and video games but I sure do like sex."

"And to what lengths do you go to get it?"

"Do they have a yard stick to measure that? I've got a yard stick that you could use," he said.

Ignoring him, she said, "I would hope that you give that some thought, because all too often it can be very destructive, causing long term damage, without consideration of who gets hurt. Still reading from her notes, she said, "Conquering any addiction, including the need to have constant sex, takes time and determination. And as with the ones that I had just mentioned the desire never really leaves your body. All it might take is a brush of a hand over your breasts, a stranger flashing you a smile, a touch on your arm and that craving might be renewed. It might only take the right word or a brush against another person in an elevator. Even your own hand may stir a desire or perhaps a click of a button to get online. It can be a scary place to be," she said, without much emotion. It was more than clear that she didn't believe one word of what she was saying. It sounded like preaching.

She paused, expecting Kenneth to say something. He simply smiled and stroked his hand over his cock. It was clear to her that he had the beginnings of an erection. She continued, "One also has to be aware of the risk factors."

"Risk factors?" he asked, surprised, turning towards her. "How can anything so pleasurable carry a risk?"

"Sex addiction can make one depressed. Or one may take on obsessive-compulsive tendencies. And of course the least considered risks are the sexually transmitted diseases. Do you use a condom when with someone other than Jessica?"

"Heavens no, it isn't the same. One loses that slick feel of skin on skin. Here let me show you," he said, quickly swinging his feet from the sofa. "Do you have a plastic bag?"

"Yes, I suppose I do," she said, getting up and taking a sandwich bag from her briefcase, not realizing that she had lost complete control of the session.

He moved a chair and sat across from her. "See here," he said taking her palm in his. He ran his thumb ever so softly against the inside of her hand and her senses tingled. "Now, see the difference," he said, putting the plastic in her palm and stroking it. He removed it and caressed her hand again, looking into her eyes.

Her nipples hardened as he continued to stroke her hand. At last she drew it away, although in her heart she didn't want to.

"There, that is enough for today," she said, jerking her glasses from her face and standing behind her chair, wanting to separate them with a solid object. She held her glasses by one hand and swung them in a circular pattern when she said, "If you'd like another appointment you may book it with my secretary."

"I'd like that,' he said, getting up and taking her hand in his. "I think that you're going to be able to help me a great deal." He released her hand though he didn't want to, feeling an emotion that was strangely different. It was so unlike anything that he had felt before that he could not credit it to simply wanting sex. He wondered if it was something that the psychologist had said. Without a doubt there was most certainly something intriguing about her.

"Maybe next time you'd like to bring your wife," Caroline said.

"I'm not too sure about that. Let's just see how it goes."

"It can be much more effective if both parties share their thoughts and concerns."

CHAPTER TWENTY

CLARISSA WAS still in Toronto, uncertain if and when she would ever go home, comforted with a sense of peace by helping in Clara's Antique Shop. On that hot summer day they had the door propped open and they both looked up at the same time as a young mother entered, pushing a baby carriage. The aisles were much too narrow to accommodate the stroller so she parked it near the door. Clara recognized her but Clarissa had no way of knowing that the woman came to the shop frequently admiring the treasures that lined the shelves and left without a word. She took her baby out of the buggy and held it in her arms as she walked up and down the aisles. It was obviously a little girl for she wore a lovely pink dress and socks. Clarissa watched as the young woman occasionally picked up an item of interest, checked the price and ever so carefully placed it back on the shelf. After a few moments Clarissa realized that she had selected and checked the very same pieces that were her own favorites.

When the young woman passed by the table that she was polishing she swept a feathery touch over it. Their eyes met briefly. She had touched it ever so lightly that Clarissa drew a deep breath for her touch reminded her of Jessica's. At just that moment the child fussed, breaking the magic. The mother cooed and rocked her into silence, continuing down the aisle. Clarissa's eyes followed her every move. When she stood near the door it was obvious that she didn't want to leave the little shop. Still holding the baby, she took one last glance around the room, her eyes pausing at each of her most cherished pieces. At just that moment a rainbow of colors seemingly glowed around her and to Clarissa it was as if an angel had been sent.

Clarissa hurried over to the shelf that held the tiny porcelain statue that the woman had fondled so carefully. She picked it up, walked to the front of the shop and placed it in her hand.

"I'd like to give this to you," Clarissa said.

"Oh, but I can't accept that," she spoke in a posh British accent. "It's far too expensive and I cannot afford such a piece."

"Please, it is my gift to you, in exchange for what you have given me."

The woman took it in her one hand, looked questioningly at Clarissa and stroked the little statue tenderly before clutching it to her heart. "Thank you," she said, "It is exactly like the one my grandmamma used to have. I will cherish it always."

Across the room Clara thoughtfully watched the interaction between the two women.

Moments later when they closed up shop Clarissa felt as if a weight had been taken from her shoulders. She said, "If only I could live it all over again I would do it so differently."

"I know," Clara said. "I've said the same thing so many times, myself," knowing that they could have managed very well without that quart of milk on that tragic night that her husband had died.

As usual they didn't go straight home. They walked through the park for it was the perfect way to end the day. They sat next to the pond where ducks and geese swam their seemingly choreographed formations hoping for food offerings. Clara pulled a bag of bird seeds from her purse and handed it to Clarissa, just as she had done when Clarissa was small. She tossed the seeds in a wide arc before returning to the bench. They watched the birds feed.

"I cannot have this baby," Clarissa said. "I'm sick with the very thought of it ever moving inside me."

"I know…. That was very kind of you to give that young woman that piece."

"I felt I owed it to her. I tried to see myself in her, clutching Kenneth's baby next to my breast and I felt like killing myself. Could you feel the purity that she radiated? If I *believed* in the supernatural I would say that she was specially sent to me."

"And who's to say that she wasn't?" Clara said, making Clarissa see a side of her that was new.

"I wonder if this is how Jessica felt.... trapped? She loved him so much. Now that she's gone I understand her much better..... I feel so sorry for her."

"One has to walk a mile in someone else's shoes to fully understand them."

"It's been a very long mile."

Clara said with a smile, "I love you darling. We'll get through this together somehow."

"Thanks mom. I don't know about Jerry. I just see him now as a big, fat lump sitting in his chair surfing the TV for a hockey game. I don't even know if and when I stopped loving him... I just feel like a liar and a cheat."

"It is all a part of being human. And people do grow apart. Sometime they just slip into a rut and forget about the important things in a relationship. You wouldn't have loved Jerry any more or any less if Kenneth hadn't come into the picture. But let's take one thing at a time now."

"Yes, I know, but it just drives me crazy because Kenneth has this great ability to suck everyone into doing what *he* wants. He's a Satyr if I've ever seen one: a shameless, impudent scheming, terrible person that only thinks of sex. Maybe inside I was looking for something......, something that Jerry wasn't offering. Kenneth, ever the opportunist, saw that and he knew how to manipulate me. "

"Please don't let him destroy you...... like he did Jessica."

"I won't. I now know that he is just selfish and self-centred. But how can anyone be so uncaring? He doesn't have any remorse or conscience. He abdicates any and all responsibility for what he did to Jessica. Hell, he doesn't even accept the fact that she's dead. He lives in some kind of a weird twisted fantasy."

"It takes one of every kind to make this old earth spin. Too bad his kind seem to outlast the good."

"Have you ever heard of the website called *Callisto Akantha*?" Clarissa asked.

"That's quite a question to ask your mother," she said, astonished and blushing.

"So you have?"

"Yes, word gets around. I'm not as unworldly as you might think."

"Jessica told me that she thought that he was doing that stuff. I think he made Jessica go on one of their little run-aways."

"So that's why she did it. I suppose she felt that there was no escape, or no escaping him."

"Just the very thought of it makes me feel so dirty and yet when he made love to me I totally forgot about it. I just wanted more and more. I almost bought myself a vibrator I was so horny all the time. Did you know that they have those tiny inserts that some women wear to stimulate the vagina all day, even when they're at work? That would have worked too. I just needed to have his fullness inside me. I ached for him. Now I just feel as though the world has lined up against me; Kenneth on one side, Jerry on the other, and this baby in between."

"Yes, Callisto Akantha," she said, revealing more than she thought. "He didn't make you go there, did he," Clara asked, horrified.

"No, not that, but I'm certain that it was coming. The weekend before I came here he invited me to join him at a friend's house for dinner. Lord only knows what was for dessert, not that I cared at the time. Sadly, I have to admit that I would have done it. With Kenneth sex was so good that I probably would have ordered doubles. It was so erotic and exciting that I just wanted more and more. It wasn't just screwing, which is what most people do I guess. It was sensual. In the end I just fucked myself, didn't I?"

"Come now, there's nothing to be gained in having thoughts like that. What's done is done."

CHAPTER TWENTY ONE

ON THE DAY that Kenneth had his second visit to see Caroline Walker two other things happened completing a circle of strange events that were unknowingly linked to all the parties involved: Clarissa entered an abortion clinic and Simone did a home pregnancy test.

Kenneth was about to grasp the true meaning of having an addiction.

Simone's test was positive.

And Clarissa was about to end her pregnancy.

Although distance separated them from Kenneth, both women feared the same thing; that he would find out about their circumstances. Neither should have concerned themselves with such thoughts, but there was no way of them knowing that Sybil's potion was at work, and that he was on the slippery slope to receiving their vengeance. In his mind he had simply moved on to greener pastures. He had found something else that was ready and ripe for the picking: Caroline Walker.

Kenneth still had that same tingling sensation in his genitals since his last therapy session. Therefore when he walked into Caroline's office he gave little thought to his short-term impotence and even less to the possibility of being addicted to sex. The burning on the end of his dick was gone and the swelling of his balls had lessened. Ever since he had first looked into Caroline Walker's eyes he knew that she was going to help him a great deal. In fact he felt as though he was practically cured from the moment that he had met her. He felt euphoric, lighter at heart, jovial and happy for the first time in months.

She was as usual sitting behind her desk when he walked in for his session, making her final notes from her previous client. Kenneth was pleased to know that he was her last client of the day.

"Mr. Lund, you may sit wherever you prefer," she said, without looking up from her paperwork.

"I'd like to sit next to you," he said, laughing. "But I suppose that's against the rules,"

She looked up, yanking her glasses off and said sharply, "I see that you haven't brought your wife," looking directly at him.

"I did but then I decided to leave her in the car."

"You're joking, right?" she said, horrified.

"Of course I'm joking. I just wanted to see you smile," he said, deviously, though he had in fact left Jessica's urn in the car. On his first visit he had left her urn at home and only for a flashing second did he consider bringing her in with him this time, but then changed his mind. He was afraid that her presence would affect the outcome of the session.

"I think we should continue where we left off," she said, taking charge of the session and placing her glasses on the tip of her nose.

"With the condom or with me stroking your hand?" he asked, teasingly. He liked knowing that he could get under her skin and he loved her smile.

Caroline removed her glasses with a jerk again and squirmed in her chair. 'What in the world is the matter with me?' she thought. She had been treating clients for ten years and never had she encountered such a man, one who could alter her whole thought process. She felt completely out of control. "Excuse me for one moment. I forgot to pull your file," she lied, picking up a bundle of charts, including his, from her desk, hoping that he hadn't noticed his own sitting there. She left the room, knowing that it was ridiculous but she needed time to compose herself.

When he was alone he stroked his dick through the fabric of his pants. "Soon, big boy, soon," he whispered, lying on the sofa.

She began the session the moment that she walked back into the room, feeling much more composed. "Okay, let's see now," she said, sitting and putting her glasses back on. "Does your wife suffer the same affliction as you do?" she asked, sitting across the room from him.

"I suppose so."

"And in the past how have you dealt with this condition?"

"I have sex."

"Do you have sex every day?"

"I try to," he said and didn't notice when she squirmed, for he still had his eyes closed.

"Tell me what pleases you. Perhaps by knowing that, we can find a way of eliminating the things that are not so satisfying, and reduce your indulgence."

"I like a woman with a tight pussy. One with a beautiful furry triangle that disguises the honey pot that's inside."

She squirmed again.

"Ahhhhum, I see," she said, clearing her throat and removing her glasses.

"I like a woman who can swallow while I'm inside her, tightening and releasing, tightening and releasing against me as I slip in and out," he said.

She swallowed hard. His description was so vivid that she could picture it. She squirmed and ground her pussy against her chair.

"Tell me," she said, "Do you find it stimulating to switch partners?"

"Like the whooping crane, you mean? Yes, I suppose I do. You do know that they switch partners to maximize their procreation."

"Whooping cranes? They're an interesting subject but hardly relevant to our discussion."

"Ah.... but that's where you're wrong you see. Did you know that when people change partners that their performance and their chances of reproduction are enhanced? For example if I were to make love to you right now there is a much better chance that I

185

could impregnate you than if you were with your regular lover. It's also most likely that I can stimulate a desire in you that you never knew you had."

"And what do you base this on?"

"Experience, sheer experience. But no condoms are allowed," he said, laughing.

"Excuse me please, we seem to be running a little late and I must speak to my secretary before she leaves." She raced from the room though she knew that Bertha had already left for the day, as she always did after the last client arrived. Caroline went into the washroom and splashed cold water on her face. She squeezed her legs together, unsuccessfully trying to ward off the strange ache in her pelvis.

She checked to ensure that the main door was locked before she walked back into the session room. Kenneth was still lying on the sofa. He clearly had a large erection for it was pressing hard inside his pants.

"Perhaps we should end it here and start another day where we left off?" she said, standing behind the chair.

"I'd rather that we didn't. I was just beginning to understand how this addiction thing works. If, in fact, I even have one."

Caroline sat down again, this time in a chair nearer to Kenneth. "And what makes you think that you don't have *it*, as you call it?"

"I never think about sex unless I'm with another person. So, truth be known, the other person is the problem… Not me."

"Are you thinking about having sex right now?" When she asked that question she saw his cock jump, straining against his pants.

"Of course I am. I'm with a beautiful woman, who has a beautiful smile and a nice set of breasts. I'd be a fool not to want to have sex with you." He still had his eyes closed when he answered her questions. He knew that he was fascinating her.

"And what would be your first move if you were to try to seduce an unsuspecting victim?"

She jumped when he swung his legs off the sofa. She was sitting close enough that he could take her hands in his. His touch was so soft and soothing that she didn't draw away. He ran the back of his fingers up her arms. She closed her eyes as goose bumps rose at his touch. His lips were soft against hers, caressing as he lightly touched her. She squirmed in her chair. He held her arms tightly to her side and had her rise. Her legs were weak under her and she would have rather sat but she followed his lead. He caressed the length of her body and her every nerve ending tingled. He then placed her back into her chair and sat back down.

"There, that's what I'd do," he said, feeling quite satisfied, loving the feel of her body in his hands.

Unable to stop herself she rose from the chair and sat next to him on the sofa.

"And then what would you do?" she asked.

He kissed her lips and slowly began removing her garments; slowly, very slowly he opened her blouse, button by button, gently brushing his hands over her hardened nipples. She released a long, low moan, wanting, needing and aching for him to be inside her. She spread her legs and he slipped his hand up her wide, flowing skirt, cupping her swollen mound. She bucked against him. He withdrew and leaned back on the sofa knitting his fingers together behind his head. At some point he must have opened his pants for his penis was standing upright like a joystick for a computer game.

Caroline saw that and foolish as it was she bent down and licked the tip of it before taking his penis into her mouth, twirling her tongue around it. He moaned and suddenly felt an ache in his heart that he hadn't known since Jessica had won his love. It was as if someone had tied a string to it and was tugging against his self-control. He felt as light as a feather, as happy as a clown.

"And then, what would be your next move?" she asked, breathing hard, looking into his eyes, knowing that what she was doing and what she about to do could jeopardize her future. Yet she didn't care, for she had never in her life wanted so badly for someone to make love to her. No, not someone. She wanted him. She wanted Kenneth.

He held her chin in his hand, looked into her dark, green eyes, the colour of moss in a tropical rainforest, speckled with gold. He kissed her lips, fervently, hungrily and wantonly. He moved her onto the floor in a kneeling position. He slipped her breasts out of the cups of her bra. Her nipples hardened. He lowered her panties to her knees, turned her to have her down on all fours and lifted her skirt over her hips. She squirmed anxiously, ready for him as he slipped his penis inside her, just the tip, then an inch, then two, before he slipped the whole of it fully into her pussy. She rocked against him, her breasts fuller and harder. He slid in and out over so slowly that Caroline felt as though she had died and gone to heaven. She moaned and purred in ecstasy. Then just as she was about to climax he withdrew, prolonging the inevitable.

He turned her over and removed her panties. He licked her pussy and sucked her clitoris. With her legs widely spread he slipped his cock into her again. This time he rode her hard, pumping against her mound, grinding faster and faster as they rolled around on the floor until he felt her climax nearing. He suddenly slowed, and began taking long, hard strokes, looking into her eyes, until he climaxed with her. Her shouts of joy filled the room.

She clung to him as if he would be taken from her that very instant. She wept tears of joy, grinding against him, craving him again. It had been sex like she had never known sex before. He nuzzled against her breasts breathing in her scent until their heart rates returned to normal.

"I…. I ….," he said, almost saying that he loved her. And if he had, it would not have been a lie. At that moment he really did love her.

"And then what would you do?" she asked, breathlessly and filled with laughter. At that moment she fully understood what Jessica had meant when she said, 'hot and spicy'.

"I might take a little blue pill next time," laughing as he said it.

At her sudden recollection of Jessica and that she really might be in the car while he was making love to her, she jumped up from the floor.

"Oh my goodness," she shouted, "and your wife is in the car?"

"She won't mind. She understands my needs."

Caroline tried to tidy up her clothes as Kenneth's sperm rolled down her leg. 'If only he wasn't cheating on his wife.... but the nerve of him, he had actually left her in the car,' she thought.

"Same time on Thursday?" he asked as he zipped his pants, wondering at that moment if he could bear not seeing her for three days.

"Oh I don't know," she said, flustered, wanting to say yes. "You'll have to phone for an appointment."

When Kenneth left her office she watched him get into the car. Jessica was obviously in the back seat and had fallen asleep because she couldn't see her. Or was it just a lark? She suspected that Kenneth was good at making up lies.

In the following days Caroline checked and rechecked her scheduled appointments, hoping to see Kenneth's name. When the name Frank Hollis filled the last session on Thursday's book she sighed in frustration. She wanted to have sex with Kenneth so much that it filled her every thought. But she also wanted to be with him. She liked his teasing and taunting. She liked how he could test her every thought.

On Thursday afternoon she was just finishing writing her comments on the last client's file when her last appointment of the day walked in. She didn't look up but simply said, "Please have a seat Mr. Hollis. I'll just be a moment." When she finished what she was writing she swung her glasses off and was surprised, pleasantly surprised, to see Kenneth leaning against the door. He turned the lock and her nipples hardened.

"Just call me Frank," Kenneth said. "You do know that by using another name it is almost as good as changing partners? You should try it sometime."

"What? Calling someone by a name other than their own? Really?" she asked, laughing. She got up from her desk and when he sat on the sofa she sat in the chair next to him. But it didn't matter what he said or did, she was on her guard this time and would not be blind-sided by any of his antics.

"The great thing about using another name is that you can do things that you wouldn't normally do." Kenneth didn't feel the need to make her laugh, as many men would try to do when he said, "How'd you like to be a Jessica?" He liked listening to her when she spoke in her serious way. He liked it that, when he asked her questions, she was flustered and blushed when she delivered her answer. And when she'd laugh he was almost caught off-guard, surprised by the joy that it brought to him.

"You're kidding me right?" she said, knowing that it was his wife's name.

"Tell you what… You ask Frank questions and he will answer them as if you are Jessica. Come on just for fun."

"Alright Frank, tell me why you are here to see me today."

"Jessica, Jessica, you know that I can't help myself. I simply want to slip inside you all the time. If you show me your honey pot I will lick your sweet sap."

"Okay, Kenneth I get your point." She wriggled. "But that's not why you're here is it?"

"Of course it is. I'm here because I was concerned about whether or not I have a sex addiction. But I now realize that it is more than clear that it isn't me who has the problem but rather it's those around me. I've been referred to, on occasion, as a choice specimen."

"That could hardly be considered a scientific diagnosis."

"No of course it isn't. It's a self-diagnosis."

"And a rather egotistical one at that."

"Then tell me that you don't want me right now. Supposing I was in a line-up of men, tell me that you wouldn't choose me."

"No I wouldn't," she said, lying.

"Can you say it and mean it?"

Caroline had never in her life encountered such a man. He had the amazing ability to take control of her therapy session. He was the patient, yet here she was answering *his* questions as if he had a right to know the answers. And, YES, damn it, she did want him. She felt like kicking him.

"Of course I can. But you're the patient and I'm the therapist so I will ask the questions. Your wife.....," she paused, waiting for Kenneth to say Jessica's name.

"Jessica, you mean Jessica?"

"Yes, she should be here? Usually these sessions are much more effective if both partners attend."

"I'll have to mention it to her. I brought a little something if you'd like to continue where we left off," he said, taking out the tickler and rotating it on his finger. Its long tentacles bounced with his every move. He placed it on the table in front of her. The idea of him using that thing on her excited him as much as it did her but he didn't let on.

"Ummmm, let's see now," she said, as she opened the file, knowing that the tickler would give her a sensation that she desired. Bloody hell, Kenneth was an experience that she had never known before! "Where did we leave off?" she asked.

Kenneth unzipped his pants and his cock sprang out. "The little blue pill," he said. "I thought I'd take it before I came in. That way there wouldn't be any delay."

"That was rather presumptuous, wasn't it?"

"Always ready to please."

"I can see that."

"I'll tell you what, I'll wear that thing," he suggested, pointing to the tickler on the table "And then, after a good go, you tell me that you're not addicted."

"Is that a dare?" she asked, liking the game that they played. And, as dangerous as it was, it somehow seemed to be too late to turn back. Not that she wanted to.

"No it's a test that only you could take."

"Am I the subject of some scientific study that you've chosen to make?"

"Hardly that. I actually quite like you. Besides, I already know the answer to the so-called study so I guess you could say that you're the student."

She laughed, "Now you want to play teacher? And I'm your student?"

"Why not? I'm game for most anything," he said, picking up the tickler. "You do know how this works don't you? See these tiny tentacles," he said, teasing the dangling bits as they wiggled, "They are designed to stimulate you."

She shifted in her chair, wishing that he would make his move. She didn't want him to leave.

Kenneth stood, took her hand and made her rise. He swept her into his arms like a ballerina. Holding her tightly against him she could feel his hard cock against her belly. He inched her dress up over her hips and cupped her crotch. In one action he removed her dress and she stood before him in only her bra and panties leaving Caroline wondering how he had opened the zipper on her dress without her knowing. He slipped the tickler onto his finger and rotated it teasingly, releasing one breast from her bra and touching the tickler to her already hardened nipple. When he took her breast into his mouth she felt a tingling feeling shoot through her belly, to her perineum. She felt weak in the knees and needed to sit but she couldn't bear moving away from him.

"Please make love to me," she whispered.

When he rubbed the tickler against her pussy she fell to the sofa, unable to stand any longer. He released her other breast and now both were riding over her bra. He then removed her panties and slipped the tickler over his cock. He took her hand. She rose and they moved to the chair, pulling her onto his lap, to his favorite position. Without hesitation she rose over him. He guided her slowly over his hard penis, nuzzling his face against her breasts. He held her firmly to prevent his penetration.

"Please," she said, in a whisper, pleadingly. Thoughts of the tickler drove her crazy with desire.

"Soon, slowly," he said. "This is going to be our day to remember."

And slow it was. She could not imagine having a better lover. She rode him hard, needing satisfaction and then he forced her to slow down. It was agonizing slow as she ground against him, rubbing her clitoris against him. He touched spots inside her that had never been touched before. When he withdraw from her she cried for him, the ache was so great. He would enter her slowly again, the tentacles stimulating the walls of her vagina. On and on it went and when he felt that she was nearing climax he would hold her firmly, delaying her release.

When she did climax it was as if the whole universe had exploded inside her. She clung to him, her body wracking with spasm after spasm. He held her tightly against his still hard cock. When her breathing returned to normal he started again, a touch here, a tickle there and a caress until she was pleading for him to re-enter her. He moved her to the floor, placing her on her hands and knees and mounted her from the rear. It wasn't the slow sensual sex that they had had earlier. Instead it was very aggressive as he clung to her hips. She arched her back as he slammed against her and he took her to an even high plateau of pleasure.

At the end of the session neither was interested in talking about addictions, therapy or sex. Both were so physically satisfied and completely exhausted that they just wanted to lie down and rest. Not that it mattered, for both knew that they were addicted to each other. Caroline to Kenneth. And Kenneth to Caroline. But neither would ever admit to it.

CHAPTER TWENTY TWO

KENNETH GRASPED Jessica's urn and flopped into his chair. He knew that he had manipulated Caroline but he had proven his point and giving her a much better idea of what sex addiction meant. In future she would not have to read from her prepared notes, for she was now more than well versed in its true meaning. He had given her his best; never one to do anything half-cocked, as he liked to refer to it. He also liked to win at everything that he set his hand to: golf, business and most importantly sex. He had faced the challenge of Caroline and had won. And win her he did. But in the end he knew that they had both won. He knew that he had given Caroline a taste of sex that had left her swooning. But somehow she had also tugged at his heart strings. He wanted to shout the roof down when he made love to her. He would be lying if he said that he didn't want her as much as she wanted him. But was that an addiction….? Could it be?

He especially liked the way in which she clung to him. As much as he, at first, wanted her to be

Jessica he knew that she was different. His and Jessica's love gradually grew from their fondness of each other from their school days onwards. With Caroline he had had to reel her in like a fish on a hook, fighting him all the way. And oh, what a joy, when she opened her mouth and took the bait.

Even now, after almost two hours of making love to Caroline he could only think about doing it again. He thought about how dramatic he must have appeared to her: standing tall and ready. Even he knew how theatrical he looked. What had pleased him was that he had made her climax so many times. He wondered if she had ever had an orgasm before. It made him feel good knowing that it was his touch that had given her the joy that every woman deserves. His touch and his hard piston. He wanted her again. He wanted the feel of her pussy convulsing against him, milking his every drop of semen. He fleetingly wondered if his addiction could be attached to just one person at a time, then brushed that thought aside because he knew that he was also still addicted to Jessica.

He clutched Jessica's urn in his hand, slipped his pants down and rubbed the cool metal over his cock. At first he wanted Caroline to be Jessica but in the end he didn't care. Once they got going at it she hadn't said a word, just moaned and groaned. Tossing Jessica's urn aside he zipped his pants and took Caroline's business card out of his wallet. He smiled when he saw that her emergency number was there. Well if ever there was an emergency it was now. He was tempted to phone her right away. Maybe they could meet somewhere?

Flipping the card aside he tried to convince himself that it wasn't Caroline that he needed, that anyone would do. He signed onto the Callisto Akantha website, looking for a way to contact Simone. It had pleased him when she had been more than willing to be Jessica. She looked so much like her and she behaved so much like her that he felt like he was with Jessica. He searched the website looking for an option of doing a name search. When he couldn't find one he used the contact link and sent off an email stating that he was looking for Simone, last name unknown, who had attended the annual week's retreat. Almost immediately he got a reply stating that registrants' information was confidential. He slammed his fist against the desk and sent off a text message to Clarissa. He tried to convince himself that even she would suffice, knowing full well who he *needed* and *wanted*, was Caroline. He waited a full five minutes without a reply, assuming that she must still be away. He unzipped his pants and his cock stood tall and proud. He rolled Jessica's urn against his nakedness. "Ahhhh my Jessica," he said closing his eyes and thinking of Caroline.

****

Clarissa, still in Toronto, was an emotional wreck.

"What kind of a person am I?" Clarissa asked her mother, sobs wracking her body.

"You are a good, smart, loving person," Clara said, as she rubbed her back and hugged her.

"I just killed a baby. I usually can't even kill a bug. I'm a liar, a cheat and a terrible person."

"It was a thing. Not a life. Not a baby. Not a anything. A few cells, little more than his sperm," her mother said.

"I know," she howled the words, "But how am I ever going to be able to look in the mirror after today?"

"What you did was right. It is done and it is what Jessica would have wanted. She would not have wanted your life to be destroyed because of one bad judgement call."

"Oh mom, I don't know what I'm going to do?"

"When you're well enough you're going to go home and you're going to have a good long talk with Jerry. You might even see him differently after this. Then you're going to phone Sybil and Sue. I think you have some fences to repair."

"I don't know if I can do that. They will hate me. They probably already do."

"No they won't. You need each other, more than you know. Pyramid power, remember? You've been telling me, ever since you were just little, that there is nothing like having kindred spirits. You have that in your friends."

"But how can I tell them?"

"You don't have to."

"They know don't they."

"Of course they don't. But they probably suspect. Actions speak louder than words. By now they know that you're here and it wasn't you who told them."

"I should phone them right now."

"I think you should give it a few days. For now you just rest."

"I wish that I had checked his cell phone that day. I know damned well that he had Jessica doing stuff that she didn't want to do. It was – *all sunny days* – she told me. It was hardly that, was it? If I had checked, Jessica wouldn't be dead and I wouldn't be in this mess right now, would I?"

"You couldn't have changed the outcome if you had checked his phone. Inside your heart you know that."

"You're right. I can now understand why Jessica wandered off in the woods, alone, in the middle of the night and in a snowstorm. She was looking for answers and felt as though she didn't have anyone to talk to. She was too afraid to tell us what they had been doing. She thought that she would lose our love. But in the end we lost her," Clarissa cried.

"Time heals all wounds, my dear… but there are always scars left behind as a reminder."

****

Simone looked out the window of her Tulsa, Oklahoma apartment. She hugged her arms tightly against herself and rocked back and forth, singing a lullaby to herself. Ever since she had come home from the Callisto Akantha retreat she had begun doing the home pregnancy test, even though she knew that she had to wait at least four weeks. She knew that she should phone Sandra, her best friend, to tell her that she was pregnant. But right then she just wanted to enjoy the experience on her own, even though they had been friends since grade school. Sandra, unlike Simone, was dark haired and dark skinned, and a bit frumpy. But Sandra didn't care what she looked like. In fact she boasted that it was because of her weight that she was so jolly all the time. She would tease. "Hadn't you noticed, all fat people are happy? If not, we would probably all be slitting our wrists. So its suicide, or order-up another dish of fries and happiness," she'd say, and then she'd laugh.

Simone would tease back and say, "You're happy all the time because you have me as your friend."

And she was right. Simone made Sandra's life very special.

Every time Simone did the home pregnancy test she prayed like she never had before as she waited for the little blue line to slowly creep up the test stick. When the blue line suddenly stopped short of the control line she knew that she would not stay in Tulsa and it wasn't just because the city lay in the heart of Tornado Alley. Of course she wanted to raise her child in a place that was safe, but she also wanted to live where everyone knew their neighbors and where she might offer a better life to her child. Names of places flitted through her mind and in the end she spontaneously decided on the state of Maine, wanting to be near the sea. She knew that she would always be considered a stranger there, but it didn't matter. In fact she almost welcomed it.

From her apartment window she could look down Eleventh Street and see a dozen art deco style buildings. As much as she liked the view she would gladly forego it in exchange for a view of the sea. Anxious as she was to relocate, she decided that she would stay for Tulsa's Oktoberfest for it was her favorite time of the year, plus it would also give her time to arrange for her transfer through work. That too was exciting, for instead of talking about oil money she would see clients who had buckets of old money, money that had been passed from generation to generation and was so old that one could smell it.

With her emotions flitting back and forth she was suddenly anxious to share her news. She picked up the phone and dialed Sandra's number.

She picked up on the second ring.

"Guess what would make me the happiest person in the whole wide world," Simone said, spreading her one free arm widely, even though Sandra could not see her.

"You've been offered early retirement?"
"No, but I'm going to apply for a transfer."
"A transfer?"
"Yes, through the bank."
"Why?"

"I'm pregnant," she shouted, jumping up and down.

"Really! Oh my God, how did that happen?"

"Well, I'd say it was a bit of jiggy-jiggy push-push and whammo I'm pregnant."

"When? Where? So who's the guy?"

"Some Kenneth guy who I met at the Callisto Akantha retreat. You said I'd meet someone and I did. I'm so glad that you talked me into that."

"Say, this calls for a celebration. I guess we'll skip the champagne since you're pregnant but how about I spring for Chinese? I'll pick it up and be right over."

"I knew you'd be as happy as I am."

Simone laid out the dinner plates and poured two glasses of sparkling water while she waited for Sandra to arrive. She couldn't get the lullaby 'Rock-a-by-baby' out of her head, so she simply hummed along with it.

"See I told you," Sandra said, jumping up and down as she arrived, her arms full of take-away.

"I guess you did. And I doubted you. Remember how I almost didn't go because I was terrified that I would be expected to take part in all that sex crap. You wouldn't believe what they do at those things."

"Probably not, but that's for another night's entertainment. Tell me about him. What did he look like? What did he say to you? What did he do to you? And why hadn't you told me before?" Sandra asked, laughing.

"Well, truthfully, I didn't want to jinx it and when I was with him it was pretty weird. He insisted on calling me Jessica the whole time we were *doing it*. But who the hell was I to complain. He could have called me The Woman in the Moon for all I cared. When he whipped that thing out I almost fainted."

"I didn't mean his *thing*. Tell me about him? Tall? Short? Dark? Fair? Come on, you know I want all the stuff. Was he nice?"

"He was more than nice. In fact he was tripping all over himself just to talk to me."

"Really. I wish that I looked like you; you always get the cream."

"Sweet cream. And my God, what a lover! And I thought that I was pretty savvy when it comes to sex, but, holy shit, he taught me a thing or two."

"Maybe a keeper?"

"No way. I don't need anyone. I wouldn't be the first single mother and lucky me I didn't have to go through a divorce or a dead husband. Mind you I suppose those two could go together if you do it in that order," she said, laughing. "Besides I most certainly don't want him. He got all spaced out when I was leaving. I think he actually thought that I was this Jessica person. He was weeping and saying that he couldn't live without me and all that nonsense," she said, holding her hand up as if warding off something evil. "But either way I don't care. I got what I wanted," she smiled, patting her tummy.

"So, tell me what you liked best about him."

"Certainly his good looks, his charm and his confidence I guess. And of course we can't forget about the sex part. I don't know how he did it but, holy Toledo, I felt like begging him for more. But I was actually scared when he went berserk. The moment that I was in cell range I cancelled my membership with Callisto Akantha so he couldn't find me. He was way too strange for me."

"You didn't even register under your own name anyway, so what's the worry? And we went to that dive of an internet café so that you weren't using your own IP address."

"I'm not taking any chances," she said, rubbing her tummy. "I've also decided to move."

"Move into a bigger apartment?"

"No out of Oklahoma."

"Why?"

"Security. I don't need him ever to find me and besides I don't much like the idea of subjecting my baby to the Tornado Alley of North America. I want my baby to smell the salty sea air, to feel the sun on its face and the wind in its hair."

"But what about us?"

"We can still visit and what's tying you down here? Come with me."

"So where will you go?"

"Maine."

"Maine? What did you do pick up a dart, toss it at a map and decide to go wherever it landed?"

"Of course not."

"Where in Maine?"

"I don't know yet. I haven't decided. But certainly where I can see the ocean."

"But they call everybody from away *strangers*," she said, trying to convince her to stay.

"So they do," Simone said, smiling. "I kind of like it."

CHAPTER TWENTY THREE

KENNETH HAD masturbated against Jessica's urn but it wasn't enough. He then phoned the emergency number on Caroline's card. As much as he wanted Caroline he couldn't understand the aching need that she had created in him. It was new to him and, after all the women that he had had sex with, he wondered why her, and why now? She picked up on the second ring.

"Hey, I'll be Frank with you if you'll be Jessica with me," he said, laughing.

His laugh was contagious and it made her smile, knowing straight away that it was Kenneth. "Is this an emergency?" she asked.

"What do you think?"

"Maybe you should go to the hospital. They have qualified staff to help you at the emergency department."

"They can hardly deal with my dilemma. It takes a woman like you. You've got exactly what I need."

"It's much too late to make a house call," she said, using all the willpower that she had trying not to cave in and agree to see him.

"Maybe you'd talk me through my problem then. I cannot get through the night without you. I need you."

"Do you now? Is that an admission to sex addiction?"

"I didn't say that I needed sex. I can get that anywhere. I need *you*," he said.

"I don't usually give telephone therapy," walking to her home office, while she spoke with him. At that moment she knew that she would comply but she was enjoying their little game. "Tell me what you're feeling right now."

"Hard and ready," he said.

"Then call a one nine hundred number."

"It's hardly the same. You see I know you, inside and out. I like the way that you beg for me."

"I don't see how this is possibly going to work over the telephone," she said. "You're right, I'll have to see you." She knew that her husband would be upset that she had to go out to see a client and she could easily make up a believable lie. Making house calls was not something that she usually did but in an effort to help her clients she had made it a part of her job.

"Can you meet me at the Victory Motel on the south side?" he asked.

"Victory?" she said, laughing. "I can be there in ten."

Light glinted from Jessica's urn where it stood at the opposite end of the dining room table. "Sorry love, duty calls," he said as he passed by the dining room. He didn't look back.

Kenneth grabbed the bag that he had packed and popped a little tablet as he walked out the door. He wanted to make sure that he was good and ready when he arrived at the motel. He had plans for an all-nighter.

When he drove into the parking lot his headlights shone on Caroline's car. She was parked in an obscure corner of the parking lot. She looked worried. He waved, indicating that he would register first. She waited while he was in the motel office, wanting to drive away, yet her need for him was so great that she could not do it.

"After you my dear," Kenneth said, as he opened the motel room door, offering her the chance to change her mind. The bottles of wine clinked against the wineglasses in the bag that was in his hand. He knew that she was married because of the way that she fingered her wedding ring each time that they had had a session. Or maybe she was divorced or widowed and liked the feel of that smooth band? He still wore his wedding ring and had no intentions of removing it.

She smiled and raised her eyebrows knowing that the moment that she stepped over the threshold that she would never think of the word sex in the same way again.

"Thank you, Frank," she teased.

"Anything for my Jessica," he said, laughing.

She liked the sound of his laughter. It was contagious and she laughed along with him.

He scooped her up into his arms, walked into the room and placed her on the bed. He opened the wine, placed a glass into her hand and said, "To your sex," he said.

"To yours." She tipped her glass to his.

Kenneth opened the bag and laid out a variety of sex toys before her.

"Well, well and what have I done to deserve this?" she asked.

"I want to fill you with sex and screw you until you shout for mercy."

"You are certainly addicted!" she said, laughing.

"Only to you, as you will be with me. How about we start with this?" he said waving a long, pink vibrator before her like a fencer handling a foil.

"Oh I don't know about that? I've never used such a thing," she said, shuddering slightly.

"But it isn't the *thing* so much as the way it is used. See here," he said, setting it to vibrate, he lifted her skirt, spread her legs and slipped it past her panties.

He inserted it slowly and fully. She gasped and spilled her wine. When he unzipped his pants his long, hard penis waved before her and she opened her mouth taking it, needing him inside her. He set his motion to match that of the vibrator. Slowly, he rocked, in and out, in and out. Caroline twisted and squirmed. When she moaned for him he withdrew, leaving her empty, wanting and needing more, delaying her climax. They had plenty more toys to try out and they had all night.

"Please Frank, please make love to me," she begged, wanting him inside her.

"Of course Jessica, soon baby, soon. I love you too much to hurry."

After that neither spoke, for it was unnecessary. By her calling him Frank, and him calling her Jessica, it had all been said, yet both were unprepared for how that night would affect them.

****

Caroline felt as though she had been put through a wringer. They must have made love from every angle. Every muscle in her body ached but she still yearned for him. She wanted more sex. She wanted Kenneth. 'Where in the world did he learn this stuff,' she wondered.

He had shown her not just a night of plain old sex, but hour upon hour of sensual love. It was so stimulating and beautiful that her memory would allow her to relive every minute, every erotic touch, the taunting foreplay and her vaginal spasms. It was a sexual experience of beautiful love making that would resurface and be relived time and time again. Words that she had not that long ago preached to her clients about their own sexuality were now real to her.

She tried to walk normally as she entered her office the following day but she limped badly from a sore back.

"Did you fall and hurt yourself," Bertha asked, concerned.

"It's that obvious is it? I should be okay in a few days," she said, laughing.

"Oh by the way, remember that client Kenneth Lund? Did you know that his wife Jessica committed suicide back in February?"

"What?"

"It doesn't say that in her obituary but I called the Blue Marble Club and they told me, or rather whispered it. I've made a note of it on the file and it's on your desk. Just in case you wanted to add anything. I also put her obituary notice in there as well."

"You're joking right? He told me that she was in the car the other day when he was in here."

"She couldn't have been, unless he packs her ashes around with him. She's as dead as a door nail."

"Oh my God, I didn't know" Caroline said, racing to her office. She slammed the door and flopped into her chair. "Dead. How can she be dead? Oh my God, what have I done" she said aloud, holding her head in her hands, elbows on her desk. "He must take her wherever he goes. So that's why he wanted me to be Jessica. He's sick and I got sucked into what he wanted. He played me like a fool. What kind of an idiot am I? Even saying that he loved me.... Loved me, ha!"

She opened Jessica's file and read her notes from that one and only visit. Aside from Jessica's personal information there were only three comments that Caroline had made:

- Tenth anniversary – Kenneth, introduced sex toys
- Group sex is ongoing
- <u>Probably</u> takes drugs - though she denies it.

She read through Jessica's obituary: two children, parents in Prince Edward Island, member of the Blue Marble Club and loved by all. 'Of course she was,' Caroline thought, 'she was gentle and soft spoken. I wonder what he did to her?' She was horrified, as she realized how manipulating, devious and under-handed he could be. Seconds passed slowly after that. What she had done with Kenneth was unethical and what he had done to her was monstrous. She sat as still as a pillar of salt.

Her hands were shaking when she closed the file. Still not fully composed she took the file back to Bertha. "Mr. Lund has been to see me on three occasions under that name and also under the name of Frank Hollis. Please refuse booking further sessions for him," she said, without explanation.

She went straight to the washroom and vomited. The sour taste burned her throat and the back of her nose. She heaved and heaved, even after there was nothing left to bring up except bile. 'What a fool I am,' she thought. 'I actually put everything on the line for him. And for what? Sex?!' She understood now and knew so much more about sex and addictions than she ever thought possible.

When she came out of the washroom she could hear Bertha talking on the telephone, "I'm sorry Mr.

Lund, Dr. Walker is fully booked. The soonest that you could get in to see her would be in four months."

Hearing this Caroline hurried past Bertha's desk to her own office. She flopped in her chair and rested her head in her hands. The after-shock of her behavior reverberated through her. She wanted to cry. She wanted to break something. She wanted to hurt Kenneth. If there ever was a moment in her life when she could kill someone it was right now. She felt used and violated. But it was her own behaviour that had had been so disgraceful. At that moment she loathed herself.

Knowing that it would be impossible to see any clients, she put on her coat to leave. She could hear Bertha, on the phone again, "I'm sorry, I missed your name. Did you say Frank Hollis?" After a brief pause she said, "I'm sorry Mr. Hollis but she is booked for the next four months." He must have hung up for she couldn't hear Bertha talking anymore.

As she crossed the waiting-room she said, "My back injury seems to be getting worse. Would you please cancel my appointments for today? I'm going home."

"Just so you know, Mr. Lund and his alias Mr. Hollis just called. He seemed pretty determined. I suspect that he might be quite a problem for you."

"I sure hope not," she said, knowing that there was much more truth in Bertha's statement than she was willing to voice.

****

Clarissa knew that she couldn't put off going home any longer. She phoned Jerry, told him that she would be in on the five o'clock flight and that she would hire a taxi to get home. When she left her mother at the Toronto Airport it felt as if the umbilical cord had been severed. In one way she wanted Clara to go with her to Calgary yet she knew that the only way to face her problems was to stand on her own two feet. And she knew how difficult that would be. She knew that she had made a real mess of her life and wasn't sure if it could be fixed. Maybe she needed to see a counsellor? It had been two weeks since her abortion and she was still engulfed in guilt when she thought about that little slip of a thing being scraped from her womb.

Jerry met her at the airport, even though she had told him that he needn't bother. He had lost at least thirty pounds and was beaming the most beautiful smile that Clarissa had seen in years. She wrapped her arms around him and tears of happiness rolled down her cheek when he held her in that old, familiar way. She remembered what Clara had said, and he did look pretty damned fine to her. Maybe absence does make the heart grow fonder? She laughed a good solid laugh right from her belly and realized that she hadn't laughed like that in years. She was so happy to see him and the last thing on this earth that she wanted from Jerry was a divorce. In fact a good roll in the hay with him would be more to her liking. As she clung to him she felt his penis harden. Maybe it wasn't him after all? Maybe she had been spending so much time discouraging him that it had caused him to lose interest?

"Come on let's get you home," he said, grabbing her luggage and steering her towards the car.

"The kids? Where are Cloe and Aiden?"

"I sent them to Sue's. I think that maybe we need to start spending more time together."

"I'm so sorry," she said guiltily.

"You don't have to be sorry. After you went away it made me realize that maybe I've been taking life too much for granted. That house is pretty damned big and empty without you in it. I love you and I don't want to lose you."

"Thank you. I do love you Jerry."

"I was hoping that you did. I was afraid that you weren't coming back."

"I guess we both thought wrongly."

"That's what life is these days, too much thinking and not enough doing. Speaking of doing, did you know that they have a little blue pill that will get things going?"

"I've heard."

"I got some today."

"I'm getting turned on just talking about it."

"I was hoping."

"So was I," she said, honestly, though it took seeing him, again, to know that.

CHAPTER TWENTY FOUR

KENNETH DID not go in to work the following week. He had become obsessed with Caroline and though he would never say it aloud, he needed to be with her. He loved her in a way that was inexplicable and he was surprised at that realization, for it was in a way that he had never loved Jessica. Kenneth could have slid through life with Caroline at his side and would never have any reason to stray. He knew now, that though he had loved Jessica she had been little more than a trophy wife. She had been the perfect mother.... The perfect woman to have on his arm because her beauty always drew eyes in his direction. And she had been the perfect bed-partner. That was until she got all snooty about the sex stuff. He suddenly regretted that he had never loved Jessica in the way that she deserved to have been and wondered if she even loved him in the end. He would not blame her if she didn't. Then he remembered the scrap of paper with the words, 'I love you' that she had written.

He phoned Caroline's office at least ten times each day for a week, using alias after alias and each time was told the same thing. Bertha was on to him early and there was no way that she would allow him to pull a fast one over on her. At first she had the advantage of call display but it didn't take long for her to use voice recognition. She actually smiled at his creativity for, on one occasion, he tried pulling off a Spanish accent, using the name of Antonio Banderas. She almost asked him to sing "Oh What A Circus'. But the best of all was his attempt at an East Indian accent, which was quite appalling. She actually had to supress a laugh that time.

He had tried Caroline's cell phone at least as many times but she didn't answer. She learned very quickly that not always did a ringing phone mean that business was good. Her phone had rung more times in that week than ever before.

Then, suddenly, as quickly as it had started, it stopped. Kenneth didn't make any more calls to her office and neither were there calls to her cell phone. He brought an end to the calls when he realized that he would destroy Caroline, as he had Jessica, if he continued to pursue her. He loved her too much for that.

Caroline was terrified, thinking that it was simply the calm before the storm. She held her breath in anxious anticipation, whereas Bertha seemed a lot more positive. One morning she said to Caroline, "Well it seems that he's got the message. I haven't had a call from Mr. Alias in days."

No one knew that Kenneth was planning a visit to Prince Edward Island. Or maybe the trip was never planned? One day he was home in Calgary, repeatedly dialing Caroline's phone, and the next he was on a plane and landing at Charlottetown Airport. He had left Calgary in such a hurry that he had even forgotten to phone Jeffrey and tell him that he was going away. Or maybe it wasn't an oversight? He was just falling apart. He had never felt so alone in his life.

Clutching Jessica's urn he collected his one piece of luggage, picked up a rental car and drove along the shore searching for a summer cottage to rent. Kenneth hadn't visited Prince Edward Island in sixteen years. He drove along the narrow winding roads ever so slowly, taking in the views, as if seeing the Island for the first time. At that pace he was more of a hazard than if he had been speeding.

With no destination in mind he drove along the eastern shore and walked the beautiful white sand, 'singing' beach. He scooped the sandy quartz into his hand and brought it to his ear, remembering when he and Jessica had done exactly the same thing. He rubbed it together creating that long ago familiar squeaking, whistling sound. Then he dropped to his knees and wept, oblivious to the long line of ruby-red cliff sides, that separated the pastoral emerald rolling hills from the ocean that twinkled like sapphires. Clouds had started to form over the Gulf of St Lawrence. A squall was coming but it was still distant, yet the air felt electrified. There was suddenly a gust of wind and on it was the scent of the storm. Whitecaps formed and waves crashed against the shore, breaking into his thoughts.

The sound of a jet-plane could be heard overhead but it was too cloudy to see. Even if it were clear there was little chance that the passengers would have noticed the tiny island as it slipped past. When Kenneth turned to look up at the sound, his shoes filled with sand for he had not thought to dress for the beach. But to him it didn't matter.

As darkness neared he checked into a little bed and breakfast where, from his bedroom window, he could watch the water lap against the shore. Just as the sun dropped over the land he tucked Jessica's urn inside his shirt, left his room and walked along the seashore. He was the only one around. He found a place where he could sit and he watched the tide slowly rise, reaching ever higher, glimmering in the moonlight as it dampened the sand with its salty wetness. The cry of the loons was the only sound aside from the intermittent splash of a humpback whale in the distance, as it surfaced and dived. He knew the sound well and welcomed it, for he and Jessica would often sit like that in their youth and wonder what it would be like to ride its back. He took Jessica's urn out from inside his shirt just as he heard another splash, one smaller and softer. It would be the whale's offspring making its first journey in the North Atlantic. He smiled at the sheer magnificence of nature as he stroked the tall burgundy container that held Jessica's remains. He felt an anguishing ache in his heart for he wanted more than anything to hold Jessica against him, in body and soul.

The sky had cleared and the moon cast its eerie glow; distant universes illuminated the heavens. He looked up in concentration and tried to recall the names of the constellations, knowing only the few that Jessica had, so many years ago, pointed out: Orion, the warrior of the sky, waving his arms in the distance, dancing his eternal dance with the Seven Sisters of the Pleiades, and Pegasus looking down, crab-like, at Hercules. The air was vibrant with expectancy as the stars twinkled and danced all around him.

In the past week it felt as though he had been on an emotional roller-coaster, or that he had mistakenly boarded a runaway train. It was Caroline's rejection that made him realize his absurd ways and that he was not only addicted to sex, but had somehow fallen in love with her. When he realized that he loved her, he stopped tormenting her. Though neither knew it at the time, she had also provided him with the therapy that he needed, making him realize, for the first time in his life, that he took great pleasure, both psychological and sexual, in playing his cards in such a way that he always came out the winner, without regard of what he did or whom he hurt. He thought of Clarissa and Simone and wondered if he had hurt them too. He wept when he realized that it was he who had destroyed Jessica, his angelic, perfect wife.

When he had walked into Caroline's office for that first visit he had no way of knowing that he would not triumph in the end and that he would become the big loser. He despised himself for loving someone other than Jessica. But, with Jessica gone, Caroline had stirred a desire in him that only she could requite. Now, he not only wanted Caroline but he needed her. He needed her laughter and her funny way of talking. He laughed in memory of her trying to be so professional as he showed her his stiff johnson. He was wrong in what he had done to Caroline and he felt guilty for it.

He recalled that night at the Victory Motel when he had promised Caroline that he would make love to her in such a way that she would remember it always. He himself certainly would. Tears streamed down his face as he thought of her touch on his skin, their growing desire and her pleading for him as she reached her climax. Her voice was so soft and beseeching as he caressed, enticed and pleasured her. He wanted her now, even though she had shut him out. He wished that he could change that.

"I'm so sorry Jessica. I never wanted to love another. I only ever wanted you. I love you and I'm sorry for what I've done to you," he said, stroking the long slender urn with his hand. Its sleekness left his hand feeling warm. He wept for Jessica and her love that he had lost. Then he wept for his own stupidity. He alone was responsible for losing her love and he faced the reality of her death and his part in it.

Jessica's death unexpectedly hit him in the face like a barn door. It suddenly came to him when he had dialed Caroline's phone for the last time. It was then that he realized he could never have Caroline's love. Feeling the brunt of his maliciousness, greed and manipulation he hated himself. He wept for his losses and for his own shortcomings. Finally he sobbed for Jessica's death and for the very first time he grieved.

Wrapped up in sorrow he lay upon the sand, curled in a fetal position, cradling Jessica's urn against his chest. In the glow of the moonlight he looked like a giant prawn that had been washed ashore with the rising tide. The salty water licked against him. He opened his mouth and allowed the salt water to splash into it, trickling down his throat, creating a thirst, but he didn't move. The sun was lighting the horizon when he rose from the sand. The tide having ebbed had left his clothes wetted. They clung to him, now half dried, and streaked with salt from the ocean.

There was only one other couple staying at the same lodgings and through breakfast they glanced in his direction, from time to time, but avoided any conversation. They could see that he was grieving. And grieving he was. His burden and loss was so much more than words could describe. It was a double blow, a double death: Jessica's dying and Caroline's turning him away. He slept through the daylight hours and again sat under the glow of the moon in the night. He, for the first time in his life, had nowhere to go and nowhere to be and cared not if anyone wanted him or wondered where he was.

CHAPTER TWENTY FIVE

ALICIA HAD no way of knowing that she would land at Charlottetown Airport only two hours after Kenneth. If she had known that he would be there at the same time, she probably would have rescheduled her trip. She had been visiting with Brianna and Simon every month since the first time that she had first met them at Jessica's parents. She knew in her heart that she was making these trips for Jessica's sake. She was now Jessica's eyes, watching the children as they grew.

Unlike Kenneth's arrival, which was like that of a stranger, she was greeted with hugs and laughter.

"I thought you would never get here," Brianna said.

"I got a new bike," Simon shouted.

"It is so good to see you," Janet said, hugging her tightly.

"Hey, don't I get a turn," James chuckled, wrapping his bulky form and arms around her.

"My school is way cool. Maybe you could come and meet Miss. Blakely," Brianne said, excitedly.

"I have a new friend too, his name is Ronnie," said Simon.

"Auntie Sybil was here and I told her all about you. She said she'd come one day when you're here," Brianna said, gleefully.

"That's right, she did, didn't she," Janet piped up and smiled when she saw Alicia's nervous look.

In the week that she was there, no one in the O'Malley household, or even on the island, knew that Kenneth was renting a summer cottage not twenty miles away, on the same shoreline. There was little more than a stretch of sandy beaches and the city of Charlottetown separating them. If they had known, they would have feared that he would arrive on their doorstep to take the children away. Everyone in their community and for miles around knew that he never visited the Island, his parents or his children.

****

Kenneth walked the same abandoned beaches as Jessica had in her formative years and found the old forgotten happiness in the sound of the wind, the lapping of the sea against the shores and the gulls' cries in the sky. He watched the fishing boats traverse the long strait, heading out to fill their holds before they made the return trip to unload. He watched the season change the soft turquoise sea to a deep blue and the wheat fields as they swayed like waves upon the sea. He gazed at the long shadow as it stretched across the dewy grass in the early mornings and listened to the robins' songs filling the air. All the while he clutched Jessica's urn under his arm and talked to her of their sunnier days of long before.

He saw, for the first time, the Island's simple life, that could not be found anywhere else in the world, and it made him wonder why he had wanted to escape it so badly. He was on the island for more than a month before whisperings of his presence became known to the locals. Then almost overnight he became the most spoken of man at their supper tables. When Kenneth rented a cottage closer to his old home, some of the retired fishermen would sit on their front porch and watch as Kenneth jogged the same eight mile loop that Jessica had run. Hardly a household didn't speculate about why he was there, even those well beyond the boundaries of the O'Malley family. For the first two months telephones rang non-stop as everyone wanted to know the latest gossip about Kenneth. Was he still there? Had he gone back west? Was he still running the same loop, the loop now known as *Jessica's loop?* And there was always the question that no one could answer, and the most puzzling of all, after not setting foot on the island for more than fifteen years: 'Why was he here?'

Eventually, he occasionally stopped to talk with Janet and James. But these moments were uncomfortable for all of them and especially so for Brianna and Simon. On most occasions they would stand with their heads bowed, scratching patterns in the sand with their feet. They had nothing to say. Then when the silence went on for too long Kenneth would continue on his way. He didn't know that they were praying that he would leave and not take them away. They had little cause to worry for in fact he really didn't even think much about what they may have thought about. It was obvious that they were happy and well cared for. And for him that was enough, for now anyway.

One afternoon he saw his children alone on the beach. They had a golden retriever dog with them. He was high above them, walking along the steep cliff banks. He found a stairway where he could access the beach and he slowly strolled towards where they were playing. They saw him but didn't encourage him to approach them. His feet sank into the soft red sand, knowing that it would be completely covered at high tide. That was still hours away. He stopped and looked across the Strait at the mainland of Canada and felt as though he was in a different country, a different world. The children saw him stop and wondered if he would turn and go back. Instead he pointed at the boats that were returning to the dock and said something but he was too far away for them to hear. He turned back, looking towards the cottage where he was staying, but the steep bank prevented him from seeing it. He said something else before he shifted his back pack and began his long stride across the beach. Brianna and Simon looked at each other nervously. Their father was a stranger to them since their mother had died.

His clothes were shabby and dirty. As he got nearer they could hear him still talking. In their minds only loony people talked to themselves. It made them even more nervous as he approached them. Jessie, their golden haired dog, lay between them, seemingly protecting them.

"They're having a ten gallon bash next weekend. It's the last of the season," Kenneth told them when he finally reached their side. "Would you like to join me?" he asked, towering over them.

"We have to ask Nana," Brianna said, speaking abruptly and for both of them.

"That's fine. If you like I can mention it to her when I go back that way and then you can discuss it with her."

"Okay," she said, relieved that he wasn't there to take them away with him. "Are you okay daddy?" Brianna asked nervously.

"Course I am sweetie. If you'd rather, I could just meet you there."

"Maybe that would be better. Nana is baking stuff and I'm helping her," Brianna said. When he turned to leave them she wiped away a tear. He didn't even share a hug or a 'how are you'.

Kenneth also felt sad when he walked away and wondered why Simon hadn't spoken to him. They used to be such buddies. Simon used to call him 'buddy' and he used to do the same.

It had been so long since he had attended an Island party that he had forgotten how jovial they could be. Tables were lined along the fair-grounds, piled high with trays and platters of food. Brianna and Simon had entered the races: three-legged, egg and spoon, and even the potato sack race. Kenneth cheered them on.

Then he did the same as Jessica had done more than a year ago: he heaped his plate with scallops, squid, prawns, cod, halibut, potato salad with dill weed and tossed salad with brown sugar and cream dressing. But unlike Jessica no one was there to invite him to join them; not that he cared. He placed his back pack on the bench next to him and unzipped the top. The burgundy colored urn stuck out from over the zipper. He sat as close to his back pack as possible and from time to time rested his arm around it. A few locals passed by but none stopped to talk. A few tipped their hats in acknowledgement but hurried on their way, escaping any chance of conversation.

Even in his youth Kenneth was never very well respected, for he had always been a bit of a show-off and made sarcastic remarks. Jessica's suicide brought all those memories back. Even then they had only accepted him because of Jessica. The small climb that he had made into being socially accepted as a part of the community and family was all but gone since Jessica had died. He was *from away* and would always be seen that way. They wished that he would go back to Alberta. He was already old, bad news.

Brian Murphy saw Kenneth sitting alone. He was head of the Island Planning Commission and

Kenneth had met him many times over the past weeks. Kenneth now wanted to build a monument and park in Jessica's honor. It would be a public park and garden, a beautiful place for everyone to enjoy and for the memory of Jessica to last forever. He wanted it to be close by the school that the children attended.

Since receiving the contractor's estimates Brian feared that Kenneth would change his mind for the cost far exceeded Kenneth's original budget. He had hoped to see him at the autumn festival and nervously approached the picnic table where Kenneth was sitting. He waved the paper that contained the estimate.

"How nice to see you Mr. Murphy. Please have a seat," Kenneth said.

"I don't mean to intrude."

"Not at all, I was hoping that I'd see you today. I had forgotten how pleasant these events can be. I'm glad that I came. And the food, it's superb, Jessica's favorite."

"I know," Brian said, nervously clearing his throat. He was uncomfortable talking of Jessica as were most people in the area. The sorrow was simply too much to bear. "I got the quote just yesterday and it came in a bit higher than we had originally thought," he said nervously.

"No sweat, let's take a look."

"It seems that it's the price of the statue that has put us well over budget. The cost of bronze has gone up significantly. But we can use a different sculptor.

There are a dozen foundries that we could consider. However this one is the best."

"Firstly, I would like you to know that for Jessica nothing is *over budget*," he said. "If I was looking for a bargain I would have bought a plastic statue from a bargain store. We'll go with it. There is absolutely no way that I am cutting cost on the most important piece in this project. I want the best for my girl. And don't forget, I want her statue mounted at the entrance to the park, to face the sea. I can write you a cheque right now. I want this project started and completed as soon as possible."

"Half would be more than enough to start and of course this is tax deductible. We can get the second half when the groundwork is complete."

"I think it would be better that you have it all in hand right now. I don't want any delays," Kenneth said, writing a cheque.

"This is most generous of you Mr. Lund."

"Kenneth, just Kenneth is good for me."

"Well, I'll get on. It'll be a memorial like none other on the island. Thank you Kenneth," he said, anxious to get on his way.

"It's all about Jessica. Thank her. If not for her this project would never be. This is the Island that she loves."

Brian walked away from Kenneth knowing that he would never attend another Ten Gallon Bash without remembering his conversation with him. He had never seen such anguish in any one person before in his life. Brian would put his heart and soul into this project in Jessica's memory, for her sake as well as Kenneth's. And a part of his plan was to place two plates, designed for Brianna and Simon to inscribe something on, in memory of their mother. They could do that one day when they are older. Until then they would stand without engraving.

Initially he thought about asking Kenneth to do the same but in the end he didn't.

Perhaps it was just as well.

CHAPTER TWENTY SIX

CLARISSA MADE a long past-due phone call to Sue.

"Sue, I'd like to come over if I may?'

"Of course you may. I was wondering when you'd call. I would have called you but I wanted you and Jerry to have some time alone first."

"I got home last week. Jerry, the kids and I have been spending a lot of time together."

"I know. Is it good?"

"Yes, super good."

"Should we invite Sybil?"

"Of course, but not Nicholas. I think we need an all-girls night."

"I agree. It's long past due."

Clarissa arrived almost a half an hour after Sybil. They met her at the door.

"My God, you look amazing. You're as thin as a rail," Sybil said, hugging her and laughing.

"Come on let me have a turn," Sue said, gently squeezing between them to hug Clarissa.

"I'm so glad to be back with you all," was all Clarissa could say.

"I hope you don't mind that we started without you. Come into the kitchen, I've poured yours already. I don't want to miss even one minute of being with you," Sue said, steering her into the room. "It's been way too long."

Clarissa looked at Sybil and began to cry. "I'm so sorry. I did something that was hideously stupid."

"Hey, we're friends, remember. Friends don't have to forgive. They love. We love you Clarissa. We were so afraid for you," Sybil said, hugging her. "We couldn't bear losing you too."

"You don't know how much this means to me. It was a dark time. And when I needed you the most I turned the other way. Just like Jessica did. I now know what she went through."

"We know," Sue said, sadly. "Okay enough of that. Let's get into the good stuff like menopause and yeast infections." She tipped her glass in a toast.

They laughed and then all started talking at once.

"Sue, what did you do to your beautiful kitchen table?" Clarissa asked when she managed to get a word in.

"Oh that? Sybil and I were doing a bit of this and a bit of that. I like it actually. I have vowed never to get rid of it."

"Okay out with it, what have you two been up to since I've been away."

"Oh just a bit of jiggery-pokery is all. Giving a special someone a royal fucking, you might say," Sue said, startling them all again with the 'f' word.

"By the way Nicholas and I are moving to PEI," Sybil said, surprising everyone with her news and changing the subject.

"Really? Good for you," Sue and Clarissa said together, diverting further discussion from Sue's night of black magic.

"And guess what?" Sybil said, showing her left hand.

"Oh my God, really? Good for you," Clarissa said, jumping up and down like a schoolgirl before she asked, "White dress and bridesmaids?"

"Somehow I think that would be a bit too *gauche*….. I got me a papoose sprouted," Sybil said, tapping her tummy. "We're three months and growing. What a pleasant surprise that was. Look at the ultra-sound pictures," she said, flashing them before they could object.

None of them had any way of knowing that Sybil's and Simone's babies, who would be born but only a few hundred miles apart, were due on the exact same week.

"I was saving the news so that we could celebrate together. All I can have is one sip in celebration but I'm as high as a kite and I don't need anything anyway," Sybil said.

"I wish Jessica was here," Clarissa said.

"Yes, don't we all?"

"Here's to our little angel," they said together.

CHAPTER TWENTY SEVEN

IN THE COMING weeks Kenneth joined the Blue Marble Club branch on the island. There were only seven members in the whole of the island's club. When he learned that the Leatherback Turtles were endangered he set up a fund to protect their feeding grounds, knowing that there was nothing that could be done to prevent the harvest of turtle eggs. He would scour the beach collecting trash, especially plastic bags, for they were a constant threat. In the water the plastic resembled jellyfish, their primary food source. He could be seen walking the shorelines for anything that might endanger any and all species, dragging bags of trash as he combed the beach. It was as though he was driven by an invisible force. Quite often people would wave to him or shout a greeting but he remained with his head bowed, shifting his back-pack on his back, mumbling to himself and focused on his task.

One day he was seen walking with his brother, Matthew, far from his cottage, on the north-west shoreline, up by Tignish and together they searched for any endangering piece of trash. To those who knew him, they thought it odd how he was suddenly obsessed with preserving an island that he had hated so much in his youth. From time to time Kenneth would shift his back-pack, stop to say a few words to Matthew and they would hug like long lost friends. And later when Kenneth would sit upon the sand and hold his head in his hands Matthew tried to console him. Only those from their area would be surprised to see this showing of such love and affection in two people who had hardly spoken a word to each other through the whole of their formative years.

One passerby overheard Kenneth telling Matthew. "They can live anywhere from thirty to fifty years. We have to help them. They must have a better chance than my Jessica did. And look at this," he said, shaking the trash bag, "All this garbage isn't helping," he said, shaking his head sadly.

The eavesdropper dallied long enough to hear Matthew's compassionate response, "We'll help them, brother. Together we can do that for Jessica. It's what she would want."

The following week Kenneth was seen visiting the High School. Word travelled faster than the wind when it was learned that he had set up a scholarship fund in Jessica's honor. He simply couldn't find enough things to do for her. He was wearing himself thin and ragged. He had no care or concern about how he looked. Gone was his immaculate grooming. It was as if it had been hit by a nor-easterly. His clothes had grown ragged and dirty and his expensive shoes were scuffed and muddy. He hadn't been to a hairdresser since arriving on the island and with its length came signs of a natural curl that no one knew that he had. He took on the appearance of a deranged beach bum.

He hadn't seen his parents since his arrival and this fact too was talked about. It wasn't as though it was intentional, it just didn't seem important enough to Kenneth to take him away from what he felt he had to do for Jessica. On more than one occasion Janie would stand half way along their driveway and watch for Kenneth as he jogged past their place, on Jessica's Loop. As much as she wanted Kenneth to stop in and see her, she never once sat at the end of the drive as she had done on the day when she invited Jessica in to tea. In all honesty, she didn't know what she would say to him if he stopped. Then on one day she waved to him, for she knew that it was time to talk, but he either didn't see her or chose not to respond, for he simply continued on his way.

Early one morning Janie decided that it was time for a mother-son talk so she walked over to the cottage where Kenneth was staying. If gossip was right she knew that there was a good chance that he was on a beach somewhere, so she packed a lunch and placed it in her shoulder bag, having decided that she would stay and wait for him, regardless of how long it took for him to return. When she arrived she had knocked a number of times but didn't get an answer. She tried the door and since it wasn't locked she opened it and shouted for him. As expected he wasn't anywhere around. She walked to the cliff side. It was warm, even for that time of year. She squeezed the blossoms of the lupins hoping for even a hint of that peppery smell that would fill the air when they were at their best. Although they had long since gone off they still released a suggestion of what she sought. She found a place to sit in the shadow of a pine tree and took out a book. It mattered not to her if he returned in one hour or in five. She loved watching the fishing boats traverse the Northumberland Strait and especially liked knowing that her husband Bruce was among them. He had gotten cantankerous in his old age and for years now he had become even more difficult to live with. Moments like this were her haven, one way of keeping her sanity. It also gave her time to do some reflecting.

  She thought of Jessica's last visit home, before she made that decision to end her life. Janie often wished that she had pressured her into staying. She, like all the others, wished that Jessica had stayed for there was no doubt that she would be alive today if she had. Maybe their problems were something that they could have talked through? Although Kenneth was not the image of his father he had the same temperament and a strange way of thinking about and seeing things. They always wanted things done their way.

  She noticed that a family was walking up the beach towards her, far below the sheer banks. At first they were but tiny specks, moving along, growing ever larger with time, like a flower opening in a time lapse sequence. Until suddenly they took on human shapes and their jolly voices echoed off the cliff banks. They had a dog with them and it was leading the way. Though she didn't recognize the family the route must have been familiar to the dog for he would run ahead and jump playfully as if begging them to follow.

The family had long since retraced their steps when sun crept higher until it was fully overhead and the sand beach was fully covered. In the heat of the day Janie moved again, to get out of the full sunshine, clockwise around the tree, moving like the hands of a timepiece. She ate her lunch and watched the tide rising, reaching its maximum height before it went slack. Gossip had it that Kenneth would often times spend days and nights out on the beach, doing what? the good Lord only knew. She waited and read her book. When she had read the last page she placed it back into her bag. She sat for another hour and looked out to sea, before finally relenting to make the long walk back home. There was no way for her to know that Kenneth was only two hundred yards beyond where she had sat. The tide had again turned and had begun to flow. It would be dark soon.

Silhouetted against the moonlight Kenneth stood as still as a statue and watched as the sea licked hungrily against the cliff-sides eating away at the soft red sandstone. When the beach showed itself as a long strip of blackness Kenneth sat upon the stone, legs crossed and hands on his knees, as if meditating. Jessica's urn stood before him like a monument and moonlight gleamed from it. When the sea revealed the beach fully he walked its length and stood below his cottage. He knelt and placed the urn on the sand before him. He began digging a long narrow hole, the width and length of his own body. He finished hollowing out the hole just as the moon reached its full height and without a word he picked up Jessica's urn and he lay in the hole. He placed Jessica's urn against his chest and stroked its soft silkiness before crossing his arms over it and resting them against its narrow center. He closed his eyes.

He lay like that, drifting in and out of sleep, until the moon sucked the sea back up the beach and the water began trickling into his pit. Only then did he rise. He held Jessica's urn towards the sky and said something. His words were carried away on the wind.

CHAPTER TWENTY EIGHT

SUE SAID to Clarissa on the telephone, "Guess who's left town?"

"I don't know. Tell me."

"Kenneth has gone back to Prince Edward Island."

"Really, does Sybil know?"

"She sure does. I just spoke with her."

"That might call for a celebration?"

"How about I spring for dinner? We can all meet at The Office?"

"Sounds great. It's been ages since we were there."

At The Office they crowded into a booth. Clarissa and Sue nodded at a few of the usual patrons but quickly moved on to the subject at hand: Kenneth.

Nicholas and Jerry were heavy into a discussion of sports when Clarissa asked. "So what's he doing there anyway?"

"I phoned Mom as soon as I heard," Sybil said, "And it seems as though he's got a whole lot of charity work happening and he's going nuts over that Blue Marble Club membership. He's on the beach every day, according to the local know-it-alls, and is picking up trash and stuff."

"Well that relieves some of my guilt for having sponsored him," Clarissa said.

They took Clarissa's hands in theirs. "Hey it's okay," they said together.

"I know, it's just so hard sometimes," Clarissa said, tears forming.

Sybil looked at Sue and asked, anxious to cheer Clarissa up, "Should we tell her?"

"What? What have you two done?" Clarissa asked.

"I think we should tell her," Sue said. "We've waited long enough. We would have told you sooner but I didn't want to do it too soon. I was afraid that we'd break the incantation."

"Incantation? What the hell is that?" Clarissa asked, puzzled.

"Well, we kind of put a hex on Kenneth. And we did a bit of hocus-pocus for your benefit too. It was Sue's idea," Sybil said. "We just wanted you to come home," she added apologetically.

Clarissa laughed heartily right from her belly. She said, "So that's what it was. I thought that I was either seeing things or going crazy. You did it. You… two… did… it," she said, and began telling her story. "I met this woman. Well I didn't actually meet her but she was in my mom's shop, and when she was leaving there was this most amazing colour of light all around her. It was so beautiful. I knew right then that I had been away too long and had to come home," Clarissa said, not telling the whole truth of why she was away. "I love you so much. I just wish that I had been there for whatever it was that you did. Oh my God, you two are amazing. Mom was right, you are kindred spirits and maybe there is pyramid power," Clarissa said.

"You actually saw that. I'm good aren't I?" Sue said giving them both a high five.

"I'd actually say it was more like witchcraft than anything I've ever seen before," Sybil added, laughing. "Holy smokes you should have seen her. You saw the table. I wish that you had been there."

"Next time. I can guarantee that I won't be missing out next time."

"What's this about witchcraft?" Nicholas asked. The women burst into laughter and they all talked at once.

****

Simone was dialing Sandra's phone number as she was walking out of the clinic, excited to share her news.

"It's a girl," she practically shouted into the phone.

"Well congratulations sweetie. I remember a time when you actually said, 'Hello, how are you?' when you called. You do recall that don't you?" she said, laughing.

"Oh Sandra, don't be silly and I know exactly what I'm going to call her: Elizabeth Cassandra."

"Really? After me.....? Do you have pictures?"

"Only two, but they're beautiful. You must come by and see her."

"You forget that some of us have to work."

"So do I, luckily I had the afternoon off to get the ultrasound done."

"So when are you moving?"

"October tenth. All to the power of ten. The tenth of the tenth."

"I've got no idea what that even means."

"Neither do I," Simone said, still laughing.

"You're crazy but I love you anyway. But that's only a few weeks away. I'll be over as soon as I can get out of this hell hole. I hate this job more and more every day. Maybe I need a change of scene too."

"How about you drive down with me and then fly back? There is just so much to do. Come by and I'll make us a special dinner?" Simone said.

"Okay to the food. You know that I don't have any vacation left for this year but I'll certainly be there for when she's born. Elizabeth Cassandra. I like it," Sandra said, disconnecting the call.

****

Simone had made the long drive to the northeast coast and soon found that she loved being in Maine. She had learned that the early Abenaki Indian had called that area where she lived Webhannet, meaning 'at the clear stream' for it was where the Webhannet River joined the Atlantic Ocean. Now the town was called Wells. She was glad that she had chosen that tiny community where nothing but water stood between her and the continent of Africa. She sat on the beach, near the estuary, and watched the waves licking the shores at regular intervals. She ignored the higgledy-piggledy assemblage of buildings at her back and, looking at the ocean, she could almost forget that the structures existed. The slapping sound broke into her thoughts. It reminded her of skin to skin when she and Kenneth had made love for hour upon hour. The very sound of it stirred a desire in her that she thought distance might have lessened. She felt as though her brain was betraying her body by thinking thoughts of Kenneth and it left her feeling heaviness in her heart for foolishly wanting him. As she wrapped her sweater closer she felt the first tiny movement inside her body. A tiny trail of tears of delight rolled down her cheeks. Her move to Maine was perfect. She was in the best place to raise her daughter. But little did she know that, geographically, she was closer to Kenneth now than she had ever been in Tulsa.

The transition from the old job to the new was simply a physical change, with different pictures on the wall. The town's motto was 'Proud of our Past, Ready for our Future' and Simone felt that it could not have been better said. She felt exactly the same about her own life right then. There were many highway exits from Wells, but Simone didn't have any intention of taking any of them just yet.

Each day she would make it a point to discover a new part of the town, as if she were taking its shape and molding her body and mind into it. One day she had wandered past the old school house. On another day she had stopped and looked at the long-abandoned train station and the memorial clock. She made a trip out to visit the two golf courses and decided that she would add golfing to her list of things that she wanted to do. She and Sandra would revisit the same places but that would not occur until after Elizabeth was born. Simone was too excited to wait for Sandra's arrival and she felt that these early tours would simply make her a better guide. She made a list of places that they would visit together and propped it on the shelf where she could see it every day.

Simone read stories to her unborn child, Elizabeth, and talked at length to her. She played her favorite music and she put earphones on her tummy so that Elizabeth might learn to love it as she did. She bought an antique bassinet for Elizabeth which she had set up in her room and the dresser was already bulging with baby clothes. As anxious as she was to have the baby in her arms she treasured every moment of the pregnancy, every little kick. She bought a stethoscope and listened to the baby's heartbeat. Simone could not have been happier.

****

Within weeks of Kenneth's last attempt to contact Caroline, she had temporarily closed her office and did two things. She made an appointment to see Vera, her fortune teller, and when she walked in to see her Vera simply shook her head and looked at her sadly. Caroline dropped into a chair.

"Okay, what have you done?" Vera asked.

"Something very stupid."

"Okay, before we begin just take a few deep breaths."

Vera sat across from her, their knees touching. She stroked Caroline's hair and ran her hands down her arms before bringing them back to her face. She gently touched her eyes, her ears and her mouth.

"You'll be okay. You scared me half to death!" Vera said. "I must ask though, was he worth it?"

"I don't know how to answer that. He revealed a side of me that I didn't know existed. He made love to me like few women ever know; me for sure. It was so sensual and beautiful and the most amazing part was that he was utterly charming too. The first couple of times I felt that he was doing it for himself. But that last night," she said, sighing, "It was for us. I would have flown to the moon with him right then. I would have done anything that he asked."

In many ways these visits that Caroline had with Vera were like seeing her own personal counsellor for she could tell-it-all without fear.

"You do know that Charles knows, or at least has a strong suspicion."

"Oh my Gosh. But it only happened three times. How can he know?" Caroline was horrified.

Vera handed her a mirror and said, "Take a look. Look at your eyes. They're pleading, needing, wanting more."

Caroline looked at her reflection and saw the glow in her cheeks and the desire in her eyes. She said, angrily, "He told me that he could make me addicted. I saw his smirk when he knew that I didn't believe in sex addiction. I could tell by the way that he mocked me when we talked about it."

"So, are you?"

"What the hell do you think," she almost shouted, then realized that she should be angry at herself not at Vera. "I'm sorry. I didn't mean that. It's him. I am addicted to him."

"Or the sex that he can give you."

"I ache for him. I want him. Though I know it's stupid. And you're right."

"Take from it what you can. Learn from it for the sake of others. The best therapists are those with experience."

Then she and her husband, Charles, drove down to the west coast, went aboard their sailboat and went sailing in the Gulf Islands. For years they had been sailing those waters but in recent summers it seemed harder and harder to get the time to go there. It seemed that there was always something that was more pressing. It had been too long since they felt the lapping of the sea against the hull. With the early fall, the forest had taken on a palette of colors: yellows, oranges, reds and greens. The air was warm and the wind was at its best for sailing.

She knew that if there was ever a place to do some heavy duty thinking it was with the wind on her face, the breeze singing in the rigging, the salty sea air on her skin and with the warm golden sunsets wrapping around her. It took four days of that absolute tranquility before she could even cry. And when she did she thought that she would never stop. She knew in her heart that she loved Kenneth and she was quite certain that he loved her too. But it wasn't the kind of love that a man and a woman could live with. It was poisonous and addictive. It was an all-consuming kind of feverish passionate sex-filled love. It was destructive. She also knew that their love was overshadowed by the sex, sex so good and satisfying that she couldn't get enough of it.

He was right, she would never think of sex in the same way again. "Poor Jessica," she said aloud, and though her words were taken away on the wind Charles heard a whisper of agony in her voice and looked up from what he was doing. They had been at their favorite anchorage for three days and neither wanted to leave. It was the exact location where Charles had proposed to her. He saw the pain in her eyes and wondered what problem she was dealing with. They never talked of their work, learning early on that shop talk at home was not healthy.

The sun would be setting within the hour. Charles took a blanket and spread it on the deck. He wrapped his arms around Caroline, nuzzled against her, breathing in her scent and after a moment he turned her towards him. He kissed her gently, invitingly and then passionately. He removed her clothes and ran his hands over her body, lovingly. She became aroused and he made love to her. It was a true love, a peaceful, caring love that touched her heart. She loved him as a wife should love a husband, not as two sex crazed lovers in a dodgy motel under the cover of darkness. Charles was a good lover. Caroline tossed her head back when she climaxed, and just as the sun slipped over the horizon, she saw the bright, green flash for the first time. She knew then that she would be fine.

CHAPTER TWENTY NINE

ALICIA SUSPECTED long ago that Jessica had been saying goodbye to her that day in the coffee shop. She had even suggested as much. But she, just like everyone else, didn't do anything to stop her. On the other hand, what was there that she could have done? Even after all those months Alicia was filled with guilt for not at least trying to convince Jessica to take control of her life..... to say no to Kenneth's demands.

In her heart she knew that Jessica loved her, Alicia, much more than she ever had loved Kenneth. And it drove her mad trying to figure out how he had had such a hold on her. In her mind he was monstrously solipsistic and she wondered how many other lives he had destroyed. Luckily Pascal had seen through him early on and steered clear. Alicia hadn't stayed for Kenneth's sake, she had stayed for Jessica and even after their sex triangle had failed she and Jessica were friends. Good, true friends.

But her guilt enveloped her and was killing her. Every time she looked at Brianna and Simon, Jessica's children, she felt as though it was her fault that they didn't have a mother. Maybe that was why she visited them so regularly. She felt like shouting to the world and to tell everyone what a brute Kenneth was but those who knew him didn't need reminding. Since Jessica's death the only people that she saw on an ongoing basis were Janet and James, and Brianna and Simon. Financially it would make a whole lot more sense for her to just move to the Island. She was pondering that possibility when the telephone rang.

"Alicia, this is Janet. Brianna wants you to bring her an easel and paint set when you come next week. Do you think that will be okay?"

"Absolutely. But I can't bring something for her and not for Simon. What would he like?"

"Oh gosh, you got me there. I'll leave it to you to choose. You are still coming aren't you?"

"I certainly am."

"Perfect, you'll get to meet Sybil while you're here. The children talk non-stop to her about you and she's so excited that your time here will overlap."

"Do you think that'll be okay? You do mean your daughter Sybil?"

"My dear, you're just too skittish. Just like my Jessie."

"Yes we did have that in common," she said, nervously laughing. "I'd be happy to meet her."

"Nicholas is coming for a job interview. They're moving here you know."

"I didn't know. That is good.... Good for you and good for Brianna and Simon."

"She's also pregnant. Or what is the modern term? *They* are expecting. Not that I can ever figure that one out when she does all the work."

"Yes, that is what they say. And you're right. Well congrats," Alicia said, laughing. "I'll see you next weekend. But don't bother picking me up at the airport. I'll get a car. You'll have your hands full with the family."

"And what are you if not family?"

"Thanks, I have something that I'd like to talk to you about when I get there. A couple of things actually. Maybe with Sybil too."

"I should also tell you that Kenneth is still hanging about. Though no one ever sees him."

Alicia groaned.

"But don't worry. He never comes around here anymore. Thank the good Lord," Janet said, sounding pleased.

****

On the one hand Alicia was terrified to meet Sybil, and on the other she knew that it was long past due. Strangely enough, in all the time that she and Jessica had talked, they never did talk of Sybil. Mostly they talked of their feelings, what they liked and didn't like and how Jessica wanted to move back to the Island in retirement. In fact she didn't even know what Sybil looked like, so she was surprised to see that she, herself, and Sybil could quite easily have passed for sisters.

They stood face to face, looking each other up and down, holding each other's hands when Brianna said, "Look Nana. I have twin aunties," and everyone laughed.

****

The life-sized bronze statue of Jessica had finally arrived and Kenneth stood proudly leaning against the crane as it was lifted ever so carefully from the truck bed. It hung suspended in the air for what felt like hours and the crowd stood silently, with baited breath, waiting for it to be placed on the pedestal.

And what a sight it was, right at the entrance to the park, looking out to sea. It could not have been planned better, though there was hardly a local who had any great regard for Kenneth, even though it had all come together so well. The whole town and folks from miles around had turned out to watch. The O'Malley family, Brianna and Simon, Sybil and Nicholas, and Alicia, formed a semi-circle at the rear of the crowd. Those who attended this extraordinary occasion would talk about it for years. And those who could not attend, for whatever reason, would have their ears bent for generations to come. The heavy construction equipment had arrived days ago, to begin the landscaping and to carve out the ponds and walkways, but they had sat idle for none were to start their engines until Jessica's statue was in place. All eyes flitted back and forth from Jessica's statue to

Kenneth. Eventually the crowd wandered off. Many glanced back for another look at the statue before leaving.

A proper unveiling would be done once the park was completed. Kenneth cared nothing for all of that public display. It was as if he had crawled out of his old skin and had become a different person. Before Jessica's death he was at the forefront of every public event that he could attend. Right now his entire focus, his whole fulfillment was based one doing what Jessica would want. And he knew that she wanted to be home, on her beloved island where kitchen parties with down-home Celtic music, seafood and home-made wine was the order of the day.

Janie knew that this might be the only opportunity to catch up with Kenneth, so she took her spot in the front row where she could keep an eye on him. At her first opportunity she clutched onto his arm and steered him away from the crowd. He looked around sheepishly, like a little boy being punished for not cleaning his room, and followed her lead.

They walked to the far end of the park where they could be alone yet still see Jessica's statue. On that day it seemed important to both of them to keep it in their sight. They found a rock on which to sit and Kenneth placed his back-pack at his feet. Janie recognized the tall, slender, burgundy urn that was sticking out from the top of the pack.

"Please let me help you Kenneth. I know your pain. Look at you. You're not taking care of yourself.

You're wearing rags. You've lost weight and you've aged beyond your years," she said.

"Mom. You can't help me. The burden is too great. I try to peel it away. I bathe in the sea."

"Why?" she asked, horrified by what he was saying. Before he answered she went on, "Is that why you're doing all these things, for Jessica? To try to make up?'

"She deserves this," he said, tears rolling down his cheeks.

"I don't deny that. But she's gone. You have to think of yourself."

"There is nothing without Jessica. Even the wind in my hair is not the same. The sun is not as warm on my face. Even the salt in the sea is less. And the birds, ahhhh she loves the birds," he said with such anguish. "Did you know what she was building a new nesting site for the burrowing owls? And after the demonstration to save the bees she even had the premier of Alberta humming The Flight of the Bumble Bee. Everyone loves her."

"Yes they do but you can't bring her back."

"But I have. See…. she's in the park. Back on her beloved Island. I never should have taken her away you know."

"I know."

"She is too pure. Too angelic for the big old world. I drove her love away and made her love someone else."

"I wondered? I saw something different in her eyes. She was so sad when she was last here."

"I should have known better. She is too delicate."

"Sometimes one cannot know."

"Did she tell you?"

"What should she have told me?"

"How convoluted it all became."

"Convoluted?"

"Complicated…. stupid….. crazy."

"I'm sorry, but I don't understand."

"Life is so different out west."

"In what way?"

"More ways than one can even understand. It became…… wild? Yes…, yes that was it, too many drugs, too much sex."

"Really? You Kenneth? I thought……?"

"I don't like myself anymore. I hate myself. It's true, and I don't deserve my children."

"They're okay where they are, for now. You just need time."

"Yes, time heals everything. Isn't that what they all say?" But he knew in his heart that that was not always true.

CHAPTER THIRTY

ALICIA SAT looking out over the Northumberland Strait, where she and Jessica had spent so many occasions during that one visit when she had come to see her. She had her knees raised and her arms wrapped around her legs, and sat atop a flat, red, sandstone rock. The wind blew her hair from her face and the tears fell. She longed to bring back those precious moments she had shared with Jessica and gave no thought or concern towards Kenneth even though it was just hours ago when she had last seen him, when Jessica's statue had been raised.

Janet's assurance, that he never came around, allowed her to put down her guard. Therefore she didn't see him wandering up the beach towards her. She had no way of knowing that he was seeking her out and was startled when she saw that he was standing before her. He dropped down beside her without asking permission. She didn't know that he had seen her with the O'Malley family, at the back of the crowd, for he had given no indication of recognition. Only those who had stood nearer might have seen him suddenly flinch.

In fact, he wasn't at all surprised to see her on that monumental day, Jessica's day, for whom did Jessica love more than Alicia? No one! Alicia knew it, Jessica knew it and Kenneth knew it. But he wasn't jealous, as most husbands would be, because no one had Jessica anymore.

The autumn gave the sea that dark and foreboding look that the North Atlantic had when the sun was at such an angle that it could not penetrate its depths. Alicia turned away from it and looked at him as one would a stranger, then turned and looked back at the sea. Kenneth didn't mind. He knew that she had reason to be angry and hurt. He needed to talk to her but would never admit that he had sought her out. He wanted to be near her, to suck from her all that she had of Jessica's love, for his own selfish reasons.

"She loved you, you know," he whispered and she leaned towards him to hear what he said. He smelled faintly of seaweed. He stroked Jessica's urn. Alicia saw that and averted her eyes. It pained her to see it, a reminder that Jessica was gone.

She didn't reply. There was no need. What he said was true. She fingered the ring on her left hand. It was a gift to her from Jessica when they were together on the Island. They had gone into Charlottetown for the day and Jessica insisted that she accept it as a symbol of her love. She was glad now that she had not said no.

They sat there like that for a number of minutes, neither speaking, both watching the sea as it lapped against the sand, each remembering Jessica in their own way. Finally Kenneth stood, towering over her and said, "I don't hate you for her loving you."

"I don't care what you think one way or the other," she hissed. "Jessica is dead because of what you made her do. She was delicate and you broke her," she began to sob uncontrollably.

He didn't say another word. He simply glared at her. Clutching Jessica's urn even closer and wrapping both arms around it, he turned away.

Sybil was standing on the top of the cliff-side watching the interaction, ready to intervene if need be. She sighed when he finally stood. She wondered what he had said as he towered over Alicia. When he walked back towards his rented cottage Sybil climbed down the stairs and wandered over to where Alicia sat. She took her time, allowing Alicia extra minutes to compose herself. She needn't have bothered because that confrontation with Kenneth had opened the floodgates. Alicia sobbed and rocked back and forth, tears streaming down her face, her arms clinging to her legs.

Sybil sat beside her and rubbed her back. She leaned her head against her shoulder, wrapping an arm around her, and together they cried.

"He did this, he destroyed her," Alicia said.

"I know," said Sybil. "But you have to let the hate go. It will destroy you."

"I miss her so much."

"We all do. But we have each other. We're together and Jessica would want that."

"I know. For him it was all about the sex and he made her do some awful shit. He is an over-educated, but stupid man who thinks only of himself and never ever heard a word that Jessica said."

"We suspected as much. Sadly there are so many more of them out there, just like him."

"She tried to get out," Alicia went on. "But once he had reeled her in it was too hard. She couldn't say no to him and in the end he was just nasty to her."

"Yes! We suspected that... The miserable fucker," Sybil said, hating him even more.

CHAPTER THIRTY ONE

AFTER JESSICA'S statue had been put in place the whole island seemingly looked at Kenneth differently, aside from the O'Malley family and those who were closely associated with them. It wasn't so much that they accepted him, but now they understood him. They surrendered to the fact that they might as well. It was obvious that he had no intentions of going anywhere else. Every day he made it a point to walk though Jessica's park and to watch the construction in progress. And it was surprising how quickly it took shape now that the statue was in its place. Folks had shaken their heads when Kenneth insisted that the statue should go in first, for that was contrary to the usual order of things. Then they would nod their heads knowingly for he had to be the strangest person they knew, aside from Old Billy, from down in Tignish, who insisted on wearing that wire around his neck with its end pointing towards the universe. But Billy's case was understandable and forgivable as his oddity was a result of having that steel plate in his head. There were no steel plates to excuse Kenneth.

Most recently, every day, at the same time Kenneth could be found wandering through the park then standing at the gates of the school yard waiting for school to let out. He waved to Brianna and Simon as they boarded their school bus. They nervously waved in return and scurried aboard, ever afraid that they would be taken back west. Then he would wait for dusk to arrive so that he could sit at Jessica's feet and talk to her. Passers-by simply turned the other way and after a few weeks they hardly noticed him.

****

The O'Malley family had a meeting. The only ones not present were the children. James brought the meeting to order. "We can tie into my new batch of brew or is this the time to bring out the hard stuff?" he asked.

"Beers are fine dad. I can help and I'll make my tea," Sybil said.

Nicolas and Alicia would soon understand, after that first family meeting, that any and all family matters and decisions were handled that way. Since this was their introductory meeting they looked nervously around the room for they weren't sure what their position was in this affair and wondered if they should even be included.

Janet gave Alicia's hand a reassuring squeeze as drinks were served and Sybil did the same to Nicholas.

"Well, I suppose the first thing that should be discussed is the fact that Kenneth appears to have taken up full-time residency here," James said. "At this time it doesn't appear that he expects the children to be moved into his care. So in that regard they will continue to go back and forth between their grandparents' households. So we can relax our sphincters a little. Has anyone got anything to add to that?"

All were silent.

"So what's next? Ah yes, Sybil and Nicholas, your news?"

Sybil leaned forward in her chair and took Nicholas' hand in hers. "You tell them darling," she said to Nicholas.

He said, beaming, "Yes, I would like to announce that I am officially employed with Granger and Fio Investments. It's a small firm but I'm optimistic that it's showing great signs of growth. We'll be living in Charlottetown. Ten miles away is a whole lot better than twenty five hundred miles."

"Congratulations," James said, standing to shake his hand.

"Okay, my turn, my turn," Sybil said, jubilantly. Nicholas smiled knowingly. When the room was silent she shouted, "It's a girl."

"Bless you darling," Janet said and everyone was talking at once.

"And no, we haven't chosen a name yet but you'll be the first to know," she rolled the ending out in laughter.

"Anyone else," James asked and when all were quiet he said, "Then I guess the floor is yours Alicia."

She gave Janet's hand a good solid squeeze before she said, "I'm also moving. I start my new job at the first of the New Year. So the next time I'm here it'll be with knives and forks, and pots and pans and the whole bit. I'll be looking for a place in Charlottetown of course."

"Really, maybe we can be neighbors?" Sybil was excited.

"Everyone is a neighbor in Charlottetown. It's so small," Nicholas said.

"Well it seems that the nest has been fluffed up again," James said, pleased. "Just the way my Janet likes it."

Everyone smiled and was startled when Brianna and Simon walked into the room. Brianna was looking bright-eyed and Simon was rubbing the sleep from his.

"What's going on?" Brianna asked. "I was dreaming of mommy."

"What did she tell you darling?" Janet asked, comforting her.

"She said that we were missing the family meeting. We are family aren't we?"

"Of course you are, sweetie. Both of you are. We'll take it from the top now that you're here. Your auntie Sybil and Uncle Nicholas have news and so does Alicia. Now Simon, you go up on Granddad's knee, and Brianna, where would you like to sit?"

Brianna counted the people in the room, "One, two, three, four, five six, seven and I'm eight. In my dream Mommy said that eight connects the spirit and is our strength. She said, *as you sow, so shall you reap,* whatever that means. Can I sit with Alicia? Mommy said I should. She's family too."

Everyone gasped. Alicia whispered, "Nine counting our angel. Time to forgive."

CHAPTER THIRTY TWO

IN THEIR youth Kenneth and Jessica had spent summer after summer on the Island's north shore. She used to say that it was where the best beaches, the best foods, the best resorts, the best.... the best.... the best..... the best of everything was. It was there that she and Kenneth had truly fallen in love. They got to know each other wholly and without limitations and she often said that it was because of their being so close to nature.

In the heat of the day, at high tide they would walk the full length of the beach, kicking the soft sand in the dunes. Then at low tide they would walk in the moist salty sand, etching hearts around the words of devotion they had scratched in the sand. They did it knowing that the sea would inevitably turn and wash them away. But it didn't matter for that gave them the opportunity of doing it again. They laughed and they loved and they could not spend enough time together.

Then on one hot summer evening, under the stars and moonlight, and only weeks before their wedding, Jessica and Kenneth made love there for the first time. Now after more than fourteen years Kenneth walked that same path on the beach alone. His feet pressed into the soft sand at high tide and on the hard packed wet sand at low tide but it felt different to him. Was it because too many years had slipped past? Or that the events were all but forgotten? Or was it because life would always be different without Jessica at his side? His recollection of those years flowed in a deluge of emotions; some with happiness and sadness, some with successes and failures. But the magic of long ago could never be retrieved or lived again.

He was surprised at the number of tourists that were walking along by the sea and sitting in the sand at that time of year. He had expected that he would be alone, not that it mattered, for even with their presence Kenneth had never in his lifetime felt so deserted and lonely. He clutched Jessica's urn tightly in his hand, walked along the shore and kicked at the seashells that had come in on the last tide.

The sounds of the season were in the air. Christmas trees were being dragged into the cottages. There were lights and plastic reindeers mounted on the rooftops. Carols of joy and peace were sung. As evening approached, the lights twinkled from the cottages and the giggles of the children rang loudly in the air. They ran along the beach, bundled for winter, challenging the waves and trying to escape the icy cold water that lapped at their boots. Because of the season there weren't the usual picnic baskets, blankets and umbrellas out on the beaches. Instead the island's blue, red and green merged into one in the afternoon sunlight like the spectrum of a rainbow stretching far into the distance. There was no more perfectly tranquil place to be.

Kenneth walked to where the beach ended. He sat and watched the sea lap against the shore. He scooped up a hand-full of sand and brought it to his ear, rubbing it together, longing for the squeaking, whistling sound that the sandy quartz from the 'singing beach' would make. He paused and listened for the sound of the whales but with the waves crashing against the shore they were either masked by the sea or maybe they had already gone south. It was most probable that they were no longer there and that made him feel even more alone.

He wasn't dressed for the weather, wearing only ragged cut-off pants and a cotton shirt but he did not feel the cold as he ran a thumb up and down the slender urn. The cold Northern Atlantic lapped the shoreline and crept ever nearer to the sand dunes. Seagulls soared overhead, riding the air currents and their cries filled the air.

Suddenly he was alone. It was as if the beach had been evacuated as the sun made its westward arc. He stayed where he was until the sun had fully set and the golden orb of the moon showed itself on the opposite horizon. He and Jessica knew every inch of this beach and he could have walked it blindfolded. But that night he knew that the moon would guide his every step. They had known how dangerous the sea could be and they never swam at night. They also knew where the rip-tides lurked ready for when the tide turned and the harrowing backwash of water was drawn from the bay and sucked out to sea. He cocked his head, turning his ear out towards the Gulf of St Lawrence, for he was certain that he had heard a voice, certain that Jessica's voice was calling to him.

The moon had just begun its rapid progress from east to west. It cast a white glow over the water giving the sea the look of molten mercury. The tide had been slack for the past hour and would soon ebb. Just before the tide began to fall Kenneth wandered to the tip of the narrow isthmus that mirrored the one on the opposite shore, across the narrow gap that opened into a bay.

At low tide and at slack water one could easily jump from the jetty and swim the fifty meters to reach the other side. At high tide it spanned almost a quarter of a mile. He sat on the jetty his feet high above the still water. He looked up at the moon, trying to understand its relationship with the earth and how they worked as one, partners forever just like he and Jessica were. He could almost feel the gravitational force as it made its change, sucking against the earth as if extracting all its goodness into the cosmos. It would be suicidal to enter that narrow gap of water when the moon was performing that Herculean task.

The full moon crept ever higher while Kenneth evaluated his and Jessica's life together. He thought about their difficulties and acknowledged that their problems had only surfaced in the last three years of their marriage. He thought of Jessica's pleading words, 'But I want you. I love you. And I don't want to lose you.'

He said, softly, as if answering her, "You have me, my love. We are one, partners forever, like the earth and the moon. I am nothing without you. You will always have me my dear, dear Jessica. I'm sorry for trying to change our life. You were so innocent. I changed everything and destroyed you. I'm so sorry. Oh Jessica, look how sweet the moonlight sleeps upon this bank. Here will we sit and let the sounds of music creep in our ears. Yes, my Jessica. Soft stillness and the night become the touches of sweet harmony. Look how the floor of heaven is thick inlaid with patens of bright gold," Kenneth said, with yearning.

The magic of the nighttime filled him with a powerful sense of wonder. He shivered, he was becoming cold. And for the first time in years he felt a deep sense of peace. He longed to feel a moment of personal sanctity like that which surrounded Jessica. He knew his flaws and he felt that they could not be shed. He stood on the edge of the jetty and recalled the smoothness of her skin, the valleys and rises of her body. He raised his hand as if to caress her then he dived into the channel.

The turbulent sea spiralled him down, towards the sandy seabed. Jessica's urn rubbed against his chest as he curled into a fetal position. He didn't fight against the inevitable, allowing the undertow to drag him down and out to sea. He saw her then coming towards him as he descended, swirling and twisting in the red-colored murky water. Without hesitation he swam towards her, moving ever closer to the crystal clear vision of his beloved Jessica, his angel, his mermaid of the sea. She was so heavenly, moving towards him, her long, flowing, golden hair waving, her blue eyes enticing him forward. He opened his mouth, allowing the sea to flush his body clean of all of his poisons. "I love you Jessica," he said. Then suddenly he was swept away and into her arms. He closed his eyes, kissing her lips and clung to her forever and always.

****

Only a few hundreds of miles away, at the exact moment that Kenneth drew his last breath, Simone was woken with a wracking pain tearing at her belly. She clutched her abdomen, terrified. Elizabeth wasn't due to be born for another twelve weeks. She fumbled for the phone and was about to dial Sandra's number when as quickly as it came it was gone. Still filled with fear she dialed anyway, needing Sandra's voice to tell her that she was fine.

****

Days later Kenneth's body was found along the north shore of Prince Edward Island. He had not been missed and there had not even been a search party sent out for him. It was a lonely old man who was walking the deserted beach who had discovered Kenneth's body and who had dialled 911. The police found Jessica's urn tucked inside his shirt. He had it lashed to his torso with the costume that he had bought for her on their tenth anniversary.

The autopsy had revealed no drugs or alcohol and his death certificate indicated that the cause of death was drowning. There was also a lot of whispering behind closed doors about the way in which Kenneth had strapped Jessica's urn onto his body. Everyone knew about Jessica's suicide, less than a year before.

****

Brianna and Simon, though saddened by their father's death, were relieved to know that they would never now have to leave their Island... Mommy's Island.

No one was more surprised to see Kenneth's picture splashed over the television screen than Simone. That day she rushed out and bought a newspaper. The headline read: *Multi-millionaire Kenneth Lund is again with his beloved wife, Jessica.* She read every word in the article. She was sad and relieved at the same time, knowing that she never had to fear losing Elizabeth to her natural father. She cried. Maybe one day Simone and Elizabeth would travel to Anne of Green Gables' beautiful, red-soiled Prince Edward Island, for it wasn't far. And while there she might perhaps introduce Elizabeth to her sister and brother, Brianna and Simon. But for now they all had healing to do. She kept the article.

The End.

Made in the USA
Charleston, SC
28 May 2014